Night of the Living Veg

Buster hurried after Fake Auntie Pauline up to the house, glad that the garden tour was finally over.

Behind him, in the greenhouse, Pablo the plant uncurled one of its worm-like green tendrils and delicately probed at the air for a moment, as if it was feeling for Buster's unfamiliar scent. Then it grabbed a passing fly and stuffed the struggling insect quickly into a dark opening among its leaves.

There was a faint, soft chomping sound, followed by a very tiny burp.

Look out for more books in this series:

The Big Freeze
Day of the Hamster

PHILIP REEVE

Night of the Living Veg

Illustrated by
Graham Philpot

This edition produced for the Book People Ltd,
Hall Wood Avenue, Haydock, St Helens WA11 9UL

First published by Scholastic Ltd, 2002
This edition published by Scholastic Ltd, 2005

ISBN 0 439 95563 7

Typeset by Falcon Oast Graphic Art Ltd.
Printed and bound by Nørhaven Paperback A/S, Denmark

The vegetables portrayed in this story are imaginary. Any resemblance to actual
sprouts, living or boiled, is completely coincidental.

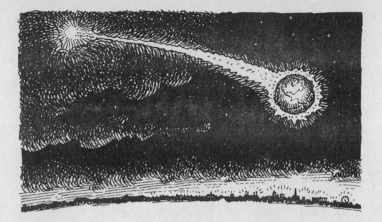

PROLOGUE

Three in the morning, the dark halfway point of the night, when all the vandals have gone home to bed and the milkmen haven't yet woken up. In the streets of Smogley even the prowling cats were starting to think about knocking off and going home to their baskets for a snooze.

But up in the sky, far above the yellow glow of the town's street lamps, something strange was happening. A cloud-bank glowed dimly from within, as if someone was moving about inside it with a torch. There was a rumbling, grumbling noise that grew slowly louder, like distant thunder, like somebody hoovering in a nearby room, like an enormous bowling ball trundling across an endless wooden floor. . .

1

Down through the clouds rushed a ball of green fire, trailing smoke and sparks and torn-off fragments of molten rock. For a moment its eerie glow lit up the whole of Smogley, a grubby little town which filled the steep valley of the river Smog the way last night's washing-up fills a kitchen sink. The fireball soared over the football stadium and the multi-storey car park, over the gasworks, over the railway station, over the deserted high street. Its passing woke the ducks on the island in the park pond, raining green sparks down into the still water. It rushed low over the rooftops on the west side of town, and at last, with a damp sound that was something between a squelch and a thud*, it crashed into a marshy patch of wasteground beside the Smogley-to-Bunchester canal.

On the nearby estate a sleeping vandal stirred, snuggling deeper under his duvet.

In the flats on the far side of the canal a milkman turned over and checked his alarm clock, and then went back to sleep, dreaming of winning the Monaco Grand Prix in a turbo-powered milkfloat.

A few dogs barked, until their owners woke up and threw slippers at them.

Nobody else noticed anything at all.

*A sort of "thelch". Or "squd".

Out on the wasteground a soft curl of smoke rose into the night, smelling of burning dishcloths. Small fires flickered hopefully for a while among the litter-draped bushes, then lost interest and went out. Soon the only sign that anything unusual had happened was a dim green glow, slowly throbbing, marking the place where the meteor had fallen. . .

1
NOT FAKE AUNTIE PAULINE!!!!

It wasn't all fun, having a mum who was also the school lollipop lady. Oh, sure, there was the fame and glamour and the people pointing you out at school and saying, "That's Buster Bayliss, his mum's the lollipop lady," and there was the chance to scare off bullies by saying, "If you don't leave off I'll tell my mum to suddenly lower her lollipop next time you're crossing the road and you'll be squashed flat," but there was also one very serious drawback. . .

If Mum had to go off and attend a special lollipop-lady training course, and if the training course was in Belgium, and it happened in the middle of term-time, and she didn't agree with you that you deserved the week off school, then you might end up **HAVING TO GO AND STAY WITH YOUR FAKE AUNTIE PAULINE!**

"Aaaaaaaaaaaaaaaaaaaaaargh! Not Fake Auntie Pauline!!!" Buster had wailed, when Mum announced her plan. "I can't stand her! Not for a whole week! All she's interested in is gardening! And her house is really *tidy*. And she calls dinner 'lunch' and tea 'dinner', and she hates me!"

"Don't be silly, Buster," his mum told him, busy taping bubble-wrap round her lollipop so she wouldn't accidentally clonk anyone with it at the airport. "I'm sure she's very fond of you. You'll enjoy it when you get there. And don't call her Fake Auntie Pauline."

"Well, she's not a real auntie, is she?"

"No," admitted Mum. "But Pauline Hodge is one of my oldest friends. We were at school together. She's the one who helped me the day we dropped a flour-bomb on the headmaster. . ."

Buster sighed. He had heard the tale of Pauline and Buster's mum and the flour-bomb before, and he had always found it hard to believe. His mum still looked like the flour-bombing sort, with her smiley, bespectacled face and untidy hair, but he couldn't imagine Fake Auntie Pauline as a mischievous schoolgirl. She was a tall, stern-looking sort of fake auntie, with hair dyed coppery red and held so firmly in place with mousse and hairspray that she could have turned a triple somersault in a wind-tunnel without getting a strand out of place. She wore expensive clothes from the big shops in Bunchester, and lots of red lipstick that left embarrassing smears on Buster's face when she kissed him hello or goodbye (and she always insisted on kissing him hello and goodbye when she came to visit, and she didn't even give him 50p for the privilege, like a proper relation). She had a boring husband called Fake Uncle Tim and a boring know-all daughter called Fake Cousin Polly who played tuba in the school orchestra, and who everybody called "Podge". Worst of all, Fake Auntie Pauline was completely obsessed with GARDENING. She was one of those people who watched all the garden design programmes on telly and subscribed to glossy magazines with names like *Water-Feature Monthly* and *Which Trellis?* and was forever telling you about the lovely sneezaria and pongeraniums she had just planted in the tubs on her patio.

"This is going to be SO boring," Buster grumbled, as Mum drove him round to Fake Auntie Pauline's house that Wednesday after school. "I don't see why you have to go on a training course anyway. You already know all about being a lollipop lady. You're good at it. Hardly anybody's been squashed on your bit of road for weeks and weeks. . ."

"It's something to do with the European Union," Mrs Bayliss explained patiently. "We've all got to retrain so that lollipopping standards are the same all over Europe. Anyway, it's only for a couple of days, and I'm sure you'll have a lovely time at Fake. . . I mean, at Auntie Pauline's. You'll have Polly to keep you company. . ."

"Podge? But she's a *girl*," protested Buster. "And she plays in the school orchestra, and you know what they're like. . . They're all sadsters and weirdos! And I'll probably have to listen to her practise every day!"

Mum gave a sympathetic little smile, and for a moment he thought she was going to give in. She knew all about the school orchestra; nobody who had heard their version of *Send in the Clowns* at the parents' evening last term was likely to forget it in a hurry. Some of the more nervous parents still wore earplugs whenever they came near the school. It wasn't that the orchestra weren't keen – they had bags of enthusiasm, and all practised regularly. The problem was, they were TERRIBLE!

They were so bad that when they entered the *Young Musician of the Year* competition the *judges* had booed them off. Surely Mum couldn't make him share a house with their lead tuba player for a whole week?

But Mrs Bayliss had made her mind up. "You'll have a lovely time," she said firmly, bringing the car to a stop outside number 99, Acacia Crescent. "And I'll be back to pick you up first thing on Saturday."

"Fake Auntie Pauline will make me go out in the garden and do the weeding, or whitewash her barbecue briquettes or something," whined Buster, trailing after her up the front drive. "It'll be like slave labour. . ."

"Stop being silly, Buster," hissed his mum. "And remember; I want you to be on your best behaviour. Don't call Polly 'Podge', it's very unkind. And whatever you do, don't call Fake Auntie Pauline Fake Auntie Pauline. . ."

* * *

Sure enough, as soon as Mum had gone and Buster had dumped his coat and bags in the guest bedroom, Fake Auntie Pauline said, "Now, dear, I expect you'd like to have a look at the garden!"

"Looking At People's Gardens" was somewhere

near the bottom of Buster's list of things he liked doing, just between "Surprise Spelling Tests" and "Getting Eaten By Crocodiles". But Mum *had* told him to be on his best behaviour so he just said, "Mmmnagrffl" and carried on trying to rub the last traces of Fake Auntie Pauline's lipstick off his nose.

To his surprise, Fake Cousin Polly leaped to his defence. She was a space-hopper-shaped girl with big glasses and a round, clever face, and although she went to the same school as Buster she was in the brainboxes' class, so he had never had much to do with her – all he really knew about her was that her tuba-playing sounded like a dinosaur with really bad tummy trouble. Still, he could see now why the teachers all thought she was so intelligent, because she turned to her mother and said, "Oh, Mummy, Buster isn't interested in *gardens*. . ."

"Don't be silly, Polly, dear," said Fake Auntie Pauline. "Everybody's interested in gardens. Isn't that right, Buster?" and before Buster could think of a polite way of answering her, she had grabbed him by the hand and dragged him out through the back door.

The Hodges' garden was different every time Buster saw it, constantly changing to keep pace with the latest fads and fashions. In the last four years it had been a traditional olde English cottage garden (with welly-boots full of forget-me-knots and a shed disguised as a gypsy caravan), a Japanese Zen garden (with swirly gravelly bits that Buster got told off for scuffing up and a miniature bridge that broke when Buster stood on it), a medieval knot-garden (whatever that was) and a Californian-style desert garden with lots of sand and a cactus that you weren't allowed to play cowboys behind.

Now Fake Auntie Pauline explained that she was making the garden "much more cutting-edge". From what Buster could see, that meant getting rid of all the flower-beds and painting things blue. As she led him from one dull zinc tub of plants to the next Buster grew more and more bored, until eventually he could hardly lift his feet up and his trainers made sad little *flurp, flurp, flurp* noises as he trudged after her across acres of blue decking.

At the far end of the garden was something that looked ever so faintly interesting. A huge triangle of stainless steel was jutting out of the ground there, and for a moment Buster wondered hopefully if it had dropped off a passing UFO. But when he asked Fake Auntie

Pauline she said, "No, Buster, dear, that's Art. It was made specially for me by Seamus O'Hooligan, one of the top garden designers. Garden sculpture is all the rage, you know. Perhaps you'll appreciate it when you're older."

"Nrrflebrrfgf. . ." said Buster politely. He didn't think he would ever be old enough to appreciate Fake Auntie Pauline's idea of a garden. He thought there should be more bushes, and a bit of grass you could kick a ball around on, and a tree to climb.

Fake Auntie Pauline led him past the gleaming sculpture, across gravel littered with the feathers of small birds who had mistaken the triangle's shiny surfaces for an extra bit of sky and knocked themselves out – much to the delight of Fluffikins, the Hodge's fat and greedy cat. Behind the sculpture stood a small greenhouse, and Fake Auntie Pauline gave a strange little smile as she slid the door open. "There's something really interesting in here, Buster!" she promised.

Buster knew full well that in the whole history of the entire universe nobody had ever seen anything interesting in a greenhouse, but he remembered his promise to Mum, and flurped slowly inside. There was a smell of sunshine and hot compost and a lot of fairly stupid flies were buzzing about under the panes of the roof and banging their heads. There were some tomato plants without any tomatoes on and some flowerpots without any flowers in, but it wasn't those that Fake Auntie Pauline had brought him to see. She was bending with that same strange smile over something on a shelf at the far end of the greenhouse. "What do you think, Buster? This is Pablo. He's my pride and joy!"

Buster didn't like to admit it, but the plant was kind of impressive. It was about the size of his fist, and it looked a bit like a small cabbage and a bit like a giant Brussels Sprout and a bit like a really enormous bogey, but not much like any of them. It was a sort of greeny-grey colour, and around the base, where the rubbery leaves met the compost, thin tendrils were curled tight as watch-springs.

"It's a new sort of orchid, apparently," explained Fake Auntie Pauline.

It looks like a new sort of cabbage to me, thought Buster, *and not a very nice sort, at that. . .* But he knew that grown-ups would fall for anything; it didn't surprise him that Fake Auntie Pauline thought it was an orchid.

"He's a very rare breed, from South America, or Japan, or somewhere foreign like that," she cooed. "That's why I call him Pablo."

"Oh, nice. . ." said Buster, meaning, "No, you call him Pablo because *YOU'RE AS MAD AS A SACKFUL OF RABBITS!*"

"He's very exclusive," she went on. "I got him from Goatfield's. At the moment Gordon's only selling them to members of his Gardening Club, but he says they're going to be ever so popular. . ."

"Gordon who?" asked Buster, wondering if Gordon would turn out to be one of Fake Auntie Pauline's prize begonias.

"Gordon Goatfield, silly!" Fake Auntie Pauline's eyes took on a shiny, dreamy look, the way Buster's friend Ben's did whenever he met Amanda Crisp from 2c on the bus. "Surely you've heard of Gordon Goatfield, Buster? He's a wonderful man! Smogley's very own Gardening Guru!"

Buster thought hard, and vaguely remembered hearing about the new mega-ginormous garden centre that had just opened on the wasteland behind the old gasworks. Wasn't that called Goatfield's? He remembered seeing the man who owned it on TV; a stocky little man with thin strands of hair combed sideways across his bald patch and a round, red, grinning face like a garden gnome's.

"I'm a member of Goatfield's Gardening Club!"

said Fake Auntie Pauline proudly. "We get a monthly newsletter, you know! And sometimes Gordon uses us to try out new ranges of plants, like these orchids, just to see how easy they are for the average gardener to grow. He gave me a special leaflet telling me just what to feed the little fellow. . ."

At that moment, Buster's stomach made a noise that went a bit like this. . .

BBRRUUMMBBLLUURG!

. . .only louder.

Pablo the plant gave a little shudder, as if he were horrified by Buster's bad manners. "Oh dear!" sniffed Fake Auntie Pauline. "It sounds to me as if Pablo's not the only little fellow who needs feeding. I'd better go and get the dinner on."

"Dinner?" said Buster blankly. He'd had dinner at school – he still got a taste of spam fritters every time he burped. Then he understood. "Oh, you mean tea!"

"How does Spaghetti Bolognese sound?" Fake Auntie Pauline asked. If his mum had asked him a question like that he would have been able to reply with a Brilliant Joke, like, "*It sounds all sort of sploshy and spaghetti-y, of course,*" but he suspected that Fake Auntie Pauline wouldn't

15

approve of Brilliant Jokes, so he just said it sounded great and hurried after her up to the house, glad that the garden tour was finally over.

Behind him, in the greenhouse, Pablo the plant uncurled one of its worm-like green tendrils and delicately probed at the air for a moment, as if it was feeling for Buster's unfamiliar scent. Then it grabbed a passing fly and stuffed the struggling insect quickly into a dark opening among its leaves.

There was a faint, soft chomping sound, followed by a very tiny burp.

2
AN ORCHID FOR MR JAFFAJEE

The next day Buster woke up early and lay for a minute or two wondering who had crept into his bedroom in the night and replaced his *Star Wars* wallpaper and football posters with horrible flowery stuff and a picture of two cute kittens in a welly-boot.

Then he remembered where he was.

Downstairs, the Hodge family were all hoovering up their breakfasts. Fake Uncle Tim was munching toast and listening to the local radio in case there was a travel flash about the contra-flow system on the B5274 – but at the moment the announcer was just burbling on about a spate of kittynapping in Smogley, "*. . .where more than twenty cats have been reported missing in the last* *week alone. . . And now Mrs Irene Minchie of Station Road claims that her beloved budgie Bertie has been abducted from his cage in her conservatory – even though the conservatory was locked at the time! Over now to Selina Packett for the full story."*

Fake Auntie Pauline was slurping tea and reading the latest Goatfield's Gardening Club Newsletter, a *Strange Orchid Special* that had dropped through the letterbox that very morning. "It says Pablo should be starting to mature by now," Buster heard her mutter. "He'll need feeding three times a day. . . Perhaps I'd better just go and check on him." She hurried off to the greenhouse, taking the newsletter with her.

Fake Cousin Polly was chasing the last speck of muesli round her bowl and checking over last night's homework for mistakes. "Hello, Podge," he started to say, and changed it to "Podgly" just in time. He knew she hated her nickname, and he didn't want to hurt her feelings, but he was so used to hearing people call her "Podge" that it was quite hard to remember to say "Polly" all the time.

But Polly didn't notice his slip-up. She grinned at him and said, "Are you ready, Buster? I've asked

Mummy to drop us off at school early today!"

"Early?" said Buster. Then he said it again. "Early?" He tried it a third time, with an extra question-mark. "Early??" It still didn't make any sense. Why would anyone want to get to school early?

"I've got a present for Mr Jaffajee," explained Polly, and held up a potted plant, just like the one in the greenhouse except that it was a lot smaller; the size of a really measly sprout.

"A present?" said Buster. "A present? A present??" Why would anybody want to give a present to the school science teacher?

"Mummy got it for me at Goatfield's," Polly explained, washing up her mug and bowl. "She says if I give it to Mr Jaffajee he can keep it in his room and the whole school could benefit. . ."

It was all too much for Buster. He collapsed on to the nearest chair like a punctured inflatable statue of himself. "I suppose a fun-size packet of Choco-Plops is out of the question?"

"Mummy says sweet things at breakfast are very bad for the teeth," said Polly earnestly. "I'll find you some sugar-free muesli. But do hurry, I want to give Mr Jaffajee his present before school starts."

* * *

Ten minutes later, still dazed with sleep and weak from lack of Choco-Plops, Buster climbed out of his fake auntie's tank-sized 4x4 outside the front entrance of Crisp Street Middle School. Polly was already scurrying up the steps, and Buster followed her, vaguely aware that something was missing. What was it? Oh, yes! Children! Usually he arrived at school just after the bell rang, and pushed his way through the peeling blue doors amid a huge scrum of other pupils. Today he was so early that there was no one around except Mr Creaber the caretaker, who was busy sweeping the playground but broke off to watch suspiciously as Buster went slouching by.

"Hurry up, Buster!" shouted his fake cousin, holding the door open for him with one hand while she cradled the strange orchid in the other. Buster hurried up, noticing with a sort of weary horror that the plant now wore a homemade gift tag which said: *To the Best Science Teacher in the Whole World, Love from POLLY HODGE xxx*

Most of the time at Crisp Street the pupils stayed in their own classrooms with their own teachers, but since normal teachers obviously couldn't be trusted with things like scalpels and chemistry sets, there was a special teacher called Mr Jaffajee who you went to twice a week for science lessons. (There was another special teacher called Miss Taylor, who taught music in a sort of shed in the playground. Buster wasn't sure if this was because the normal teachers couldn't be trusted with drums, trumpets, glockenspiels, triangles and recorders, or just because they couldn't stand the noise 2b made when they got hold of them.)

Mr Jaffajee was in his laboratory, checking the bunsen burners. He hadn't put on his white lab coat yet so he looked less like a mad scientist than usual and more like an ordinary human being – except that no ordinary human being would have looked so pleased to see Fake Cousin Polly bouncing into their room at eight twenty-five on a Thursday morning.

"Well," said Mr Jaffajee, beaming, "if it isn't my star pupil! Oh, and Buster. . ." (His smile faded a bit, and he quickly pushed the bunsen burners out of Buster's reach.) "What can I do for you, young Polly?"

Polly proudly presented him with her plant. "It's an orchid," she said. "I've printed out all the details about how to look after it off the Goatfield's Garden Centre web site, and I got

Daddy to laminate them for me at work."

"Ah," said Mr Jaffajee, a little perplexed, staring down at the ugly little grey vegetable in its plastic pot. "Well, ah, thanks, Polly, it'll cheer up the science room no end. . ."

"Mr Goatfield says it's a new species, unique to Smogley," said Polly brightly. "He found the first one himself."

"Hmm. . ." said Mr Jaffajee, groping at his sweater in the place where his pens would have been if he'd had his lab coat on. Ever helpful, Polly passed him her multi-coloured biro, and started rummaging in her rucksack for the internet pages while he gently prodded the plant's petals. "Are you sure it's an orchid, Polly? I'd say it was some kind of cabbage, but it doesn't look like quite like any I've seen before. . ."

Quicker than a jack-in-the-box, the plant opened its leaves. Polly had her nose in her rucksack still, so she didn't see what happened next – but Buster did. The morning sunlight was pouring through the science room windows, and in its slanting rays he clearly saw a puff of green dust shoot out of the plant into Mr Jaffajee's face, coiling into his mouth and nose like smoke.

"Ahhhhtchoo!" sneezed the science teacher, and took the paper tissue that Polly promptly handed him. "Oh, excuse me . . . my hayfever. . ." He smiled happily at Polly, and then at Buster. Buster started to get an uneasy feeling. He couldn't remember the last time a teacher had looked pleased to see him. He could still see flecks of the green dust clinging to Mr Jaffajee's beard, and for a moment he thought they were glowing, pulsing slowly with a faint, greenish light – but perhaps it was just a trick of the sunlight, for a moment later he couldn't see them at all.

"It was very kind of you both to bring this lovely, lovely orchid in," said Mr Jaffajee, carefully picking up the plant and setting it on his desk. "I shall take great care of it. It'll be interesting to see how it develops. . ." Then he seemed to forget that they were there. Lost in thought, he stood beaming at the plant, stroking his beard and humming softly to himself until the bell went, startling him out of his trance. "Well, run along!" he said, ushering them to the door, and as they left Buster glanced back in time to see him peering at the plant again, with the same dozy smile that he had seen on Fake Auntie Pauline in the greenhouse yesterday. . .

* * *

It was strange behaviour, but teachers were always

behaving strangely, so Buster thought no more about the plant. Anyway, he had to come up with a new excuse for not handing in his homework. He couldn't say the dog had eaten it, because he had used that two weeks running and Miss Ellis, his teacher, was starting to get suspicious. He toyed with telling her that it had been abducted by aliens, or pinched from his rucksack by a criminal mastermind . . . but excuses like that were just too good to waste; it would be better to save them for a real emergency.

In the end, when Miss Ellis said, "Now, 2b, I'd like you all to hand in the geography worksheets I gave you last week," he put his hand up and said, "Sorry, Miss, but my mum's away and I'm staying with my Fake Auntie Pauline and she's this mad keen gardener and when she saw my worksheet lying around she didn't know what it was and she tore it up and stuck it on the compost, Miss."

"Really, Buster?" sighed the teacher. "Well, will you try and get it done for tomorrow, please? And this time, take a bit more care of it. . ."

She plonked a fresh copy of the worksheet on Buster's desk, and as she turned away he collapsed, exhausted. It was a terrible strain on the brain, having to come up with these stories every week. Sometimes he almost found himself wondering if it wouldn't be easier just to do the homework. . .

"Still," said Miss Ellis brightly, turning to face the class, "it's nice to hear that Buster's auntie likes gardening. It would do us all good to get to know more about plants and the environment. In fact, I've asked the headmaster if we can plant a school garden on the wasteground behind the bicycle shed. I'm a member of Goatfield's Gardening Club and Mr Goatfield has very kindly offered to donate some seedlings. Who'd be interested in helping to plant them?"

You could almost hear the brain-cells whirring as everyone in 2b thought, *Gardening = afternoons off = less work!* As it sunk in, a forest of grubby hands began to sprout, and eager voices called out, "Ooh, Miss, me, Miss, Miss, Miss!"

But Buster, who would usually have been the first to volunteer for anything that meant less work and more mucking about outside, said nothing at all. He hadn't noticed it before, but now that he had, he couldn't take his eyes off it. . .

Up on the shelf above Miss Ellis's desk, where she kept her dictionary and her glasses and her *I hate kids* coffee mug, a new flowerpot had appeared, and poking out of the top was a familiar clump of rubbery grey-green leaves.

3
PLANT POWER!

Buster was late meeting Polly outside the
school gates that afternoon, but he needn't
have worried: Fake Auntie Pauline's enormous
car was nowhere to be seen. Polly stood all
alone on the empty pavement, a small drift of
wind-blown sweet-wrappers collecting around
her feet.

"Where have you been?" she asked, as Buster
came slouching over to join her.

"I had to talk to some people," explained
Buster. "Something came up. . ."

"Three-thirty, Mummy said," Polly reminded
him.

"Yeah?" said Buster. "Well, where is she, then? I
can't see her car."

"I know," admitted Polly, her prim expression crumpling a bit around the edges. "I don't understand it. She's *always* here to meet me at three-thirty, and now it's nearly ten to four, and all the other mummies have been and gone. . ."

"Maybe she's been held up?" suggested Buster.

"But why?" Polly frowned furiously. "It's not as if she goes to work, like Daddy. She was just supposed to be pottering in the garden today. She's been very strange, these last few days. She won't even let me practise my tuba at home any more, and she knows my grade seven exam is only six weeks away. . ."

"It's that plant," said Buster.

"What?"

"That cabbage thing. I've been talking to the other kids about them. They're all over the place!"

"Of course. A lot of people go to Goatfield's. Gardening is a very popular hobby."

"But they're making people go really weird!"

Polly looked sideways at Buster as if she suspected he was making fun of her. "That's silly. How can a plant make people go weird?"

"I don't know," Buster admitted. "But when I asked my mate Ben if he wanted to play Busterball tonight, he said he had to go home and look after this new orchid what his mum had got him from Goatfield's. . ."

"Sounds reasonable," sniffed Polly. (Everyone at Crisp Street knew that Busterball was a loud and dangerous game involving three footballs, four goals, some skateboards – or bikes, depending on availability – lots of water-bombs and any passing dogs who felt like joining in.) "*I'd* rather look after an orchid than play Busterball," she added.

"Yes, but you're a *girl*," Buster explained patiently. "I'm talking about *Ben*. Ben isn't interested in plants. The nearest Ben ever gets to gardening is playing *Attack of the Killer Geranium* on his computer. And he can only get to level twelve of *that*. And Miss Ellis has got one of the plants too, and she's gone really strange; she just smiled when I told her about your mum throwing my geography worksheet in the compost bin, and now she's getting loads more from Goatfield's Gardening Club and she's planning to start a school garden with them. . ."

"Mummy didn't throw your geography worksheet in the compost bin," protested Polly.

"And you saw the way Mr Jaffajee went when he sniffed that sprout you gave him. He wasn't fooled at first; he knew it wasn't an orchid. But then it did something to him and now he's in its power!"

"Come to think of it, Mummy hasn't even got a compost bin," said Polly, who had stopped listening. Before Buster could explain any further, the clock on the nearby church struck four. The fake cousins exchanged a worried glance. Super-efficient Auntie Pauline was now a whole half-hour late!

* * *

In the end they walked home to Acacia Crescent. It didn't bother Buster, who always walked to and from school, except when he went by bike or skateboard, and it was quicker than sitting in the traffic-jams. The only tricky bit was crossing Dancers Road, the big main road that ran through the middle of Smogley. Usually, Buster's mum would have been there to stop the cars with her lollipop. Today, of course, she was in Belgium. She'd been replaced by her friend, temporary lollipop-person Rosalie Fudge. Rosalie was kind and funny, and Buster secretly thought she looked quite pretty in her day-glo uniform, but the trouble was she was a poet, and you never knew when she would get an idea for a poem and have to run off and write it down before she forgot it. Today, inspiration struck just as Buster and Polly reached the middle of Dancers Road. "Oooh! I've just thought of a sonnet!" she gasped, and ran back to the pavement to jot it down, leaving Buster and his fake cousin scrambling desperately to safety through a sea of snarling, tooting traffic.

"I hope Mum gets back soon!" gasped Buster, pausing to catch his breath once he reached the other side, but poor Fake Cousin Polly didn't answer. She was used to being ferried about everywhere in her mother's car and she hadn't been prepared for the dangers of walking home. She wasn't very fit, either. By the time they had gone a couple of blocks she was lagging behind, red-faced and footsore. Reluctantly, Buster offered to carry her bag for her, and hurried the rest of the way quietly praying that none of his friends spotted him — he could just imagine them all going, "Oooh, Buster carried Podge's bags, she's his *girlfriend!*" The bag weighed a ton; it was packed full of Polly's brainy books and bulging folders. Still, thought Buster, at least this wasn't her tuba-lesson day. . .

As he had half expected, they found Fake Auntie Pauline in her greenhouse. Her sleeves were rolled up and there was a smudge of earth on her nose and a plastic bag full of something lumpy in her hand. When she heard the children coming she quickly hid the bag and turned to meet them with a wobbly smile.

"Polly! Buster! Oh, is that the time? I've completely lost track. . . I was just checking on Pablo. Look how he's grown!"

The sprout-cabbage-bogey in the pot beside her was now the size of a football, its fleshy leaves quivering slightly. Buster thought it looked rather pleased with itself.

"It's grown by all that in a *day?*" asked Polly, amazed.

"How big is it going to get?" Buster wondered.

"Who knows?" Fake Auntie Pauline gave a brittle little laugh.

Buster wanted to take a closer look at the plant, but Fake Auntie Pauline seemed reluctant to let them come any nearer. "Come along, children!" she chirped, bundling them out of the greenhouse. Fluffikins, the Hodges' fat and vicious cat, prowled past her, keen to investigate Pablo for himself, but Fake Auntie Pauline quickly slid the door shut and he had to content himself with pressing his big flat face against the glass and yowling. Fake Auntie Pauline ignored him and trotted off towards the house. "Leek and tunafish bake for dinner!" she called back brightly. "Come on, Buster. Come on, Pablo!"

"It's Polly, Mummy," said Polly.

"That's what I said," replied her mother, heading for the kitchen door.

Buster and his fake cousin exchanged worried looks, and hurried after her.

* * *

There was an e-mail from Mum waiting on the computer in Fake Uncle Tim's study. She had arrived safely at the European lollipop-person-training-school at Camp Kludge, and she had made friends with some French and German lollipop ladies. One of them had a digital camera, and Mum had attached a photo of a whole bunch of people in dayglo uniforms all holding lollipops that said "STOP – Children Crossing" in different languages. A little arrow pointed to one of the figures with the word ME!

Buster e-mailed back: *Deer Mum, having a horible time food is horible scool is horible Fake Auntie Pauleen is completly bonkers, wish you were here.* He wondered if he should mention the strange plants, but decided not to. Mum wasn't exactly a grown-up, but she was fairly sensible, so she probably wouldn't believe a word of it.

Later, when dinner was over, when Fake Auntie Pauline and Fake Uncle Tim had sat down to watch their favourite gardening programme and Buster had slouched off upstairs to do his homework, Polly came creeping into the guest bedroom.

"Buster?" she said. "I'm really worried. . ."

Buster quickly filled in the spaces for answers on his geography worksheet by scribbling "yes", "no" and "ox-bow lakes" over them at random, then cleared a space on the bed for his fake cousin to sit down. He was pleased to see that, after only twenty-four hours, Fake Auntie Pauline's guest room was already starting to look a bit like his own bedroom at home, covered in dropped comics, muddy trainers, abandoned T-shirts and dirty socks. He felt quite proud when Polly looked around in amazement and said, "Oh, *yuck!*"

"So what appears to be the problem, Miss Hodge?" he asked, pacing to and fro with his hands behind his back like Sherlock Holmes, then spoiling the effect a bit by slipping over on half a Mars bar that had somehow got left on the carpet.

"It's Mummy," said Polly. "I think you might be right about the plant. Didn't you notice earlier?

All the plates and bowls from breakfast-time were still sitting on the draining board, and the washing hasn't been done ... she hasn't done any housework at all! Usually she does *everything*. I think she's been in that greenhouse all day, watching that plant grow. And it's definitely not an orchid: I looked orchids up in an encyclopaedia and they don't look anything like that."

"Hmmmm," said Buster. Once he'd pulled off most of the fluff, his half a Mars bar didn't taste too bad.

"And there's something else," Polly went on. "I looked in the bin for that plastic bag; the one she didn't want us to see; the one she hid when we came to the greenhouse. Guess what was in it?"

"Er . . . some kind of plant-food?" Buster said.

"Steak," Polly told him. "Raw steak, from the butcher's. There was still some blood in the bag. Buster, those sprouts are meat-eaters!"

4
BUSTER'S MIDNIGHT GARDEN

Buster had bad dreams that night. It was all Polly's fault. She had insisted on getting out one of her huge encyclopaedias and showing him pictures of those weird jungle plants that caught flies between their fanged petals, or lured them to a sticky death in deep chambers between their leaves. "Carnivorous plants do exist," she told him, "but I've never seen pictures of anything like Pablo. And the others eat insects, not steak. What do these things live on in the wild, when they haven't got Mummy to keep popping down to the butcher's for them?"

Buster dreamed that what the plants lived on in the wild was *Buster*. He dreamed that hungry sprouts were chasing him through a forest, and when they caught him they were going to turn him into a Buster-burger. At last they cornered him and began to close in, all lashing their leaves and growling, lit up by an eerie green light that pulsed and throbbed, brighter and brighter. . .

. . .until he woke up. He was in Fake Auntie Pauline's guest bedroom – he could see the flowery wallpaper and the kitten picture, which was odd, because it was three o'clock in the morning, and the room was at the back of the house, so there were no street lamps outside. Then he realized that there was a light shining through the gap in the curtains. A green light. A green light that throbbed and pulsed, pulsed and throbbed, never very bright, sometimes very faint, but never quite fading away.

He clambered out of bed and went to the window. Below him the shark's-fin shadow of the metal sculpture fluttered and danced in the midnight garden, and inside the greenhouse the green light glowed.

Buster tugged his trainers on and pulled his jacket on over the top of his Action Man pyjamas. Slipping out of the room as quietly as he could, he paused for a moment at the top of the stairs to listen to the sounds of the sleeping house. He heard Polly's soft snores echoing around her immaculately tidy bedroom, and from the main bedroom at the far end of the hall came Fake Uncle Tim's louder snore and the sound of Fake Auntie Pauline talking in her sleep: "Ooh, Mr Titchmarsh! What a lovely surprise!"

Satisfied that everyone was safely asleep, Buster scurried down the stairs. Fake Auntie Pauline's torch was on the kitchen table where she had left it after saying goodnight to Pablo a few hours earlier. He slipped it into his pocket, eased the back door open and stepped out into the night.

It was cold, and very quiet. The dim green light from the far end of the garden glittered faintly on the dew-wet decking, and beyond the garden fence the other gardens of Acacia Crescent stretched away in a long curve. In five or six of them Buster thought he saw an answering green glow pulsing, pulsing. . .

He crept towards the greenhouse, the crunch of his trainers horribly loud on the patches of gravel, the wet decking slithery underfoot. Then, as he drew level with Seamus O'Hooligan's metal sculpture, something soft and sinuous wrapped itself around his leg.

"Eeeek!" screamed Buster, snatching the torch from his pocket. The scream sounded terribly loud to him, but in fact it was just a whisper, and none of the sleeping inhabitants of Acacia Crescent heard it. In the torch-light Buster saw Fluffikins' sullen face staring up at him, eyes bouncing back the yellow beam like two mirrors. "Stupid cat!" he said.

"Miaow!" whined Fluffikins, dropping the dead vole he had been carrying and starting to wind his chubby body in and out around Buster's ankles. He was hoping Buster might come back to the kitchen and open up a tin of Kittysnax for him – he had had a bowl at dinner time and since then he'd eaten nothing but six mice, three voles, two spiders, a fledgling bird and Fake Auntie Pauline's gardening gloves.

"Shoo!" hissed Buster. "Shove off, fatso!" But Fluffikins still slunk along behind him as he stepped past the stainless steel sculpture and let himself into the greenhouse.

The air inside was hot and damp, and there was a sweet, cloying smell that made Buster feel sick. He felt sicker still when he saw Pablo. The plant was the size of a beachball now. It had burst out of its pot and sat in a heap of soil and compost and terracotta shards, while the tendrils around its base moved to and fro like blind snakes, stroking and fingering the heavy air. Dim green light throbbed from it, coursing like neon through the veins of its rubbery leaves, and it was singing to itself, a shrill, batlike sound that dropped now and again into the upper range of Buster's hearing.

His hair stood on end, and he took a step backwards. But Fluffikins, attracted by the writhing movement of the tendrils, slithered between his legs and jumped up on to the table where Pablo stood.

The plant struck instantly, all its tendrils lashing out together and wrapping around the startled moggie like mad green spaghetti. Fluffikins hissed and yowled, lashing out with his claws in every direction, but the plant lifted him easily and drew him towards its centre, where the big leaves were peeling back to reveal an opening like a dark mouth, lined with thorns.

"No!" shouted Buster. He picked up a plant pot and flung it at Pablo, and the plant, tendrils still tightening around poor Fluffikins, dropped heavily off its table and rolled across the greenhouse floor. Buster booted it once, twice with his trainered foot, struggled free of a coiling tendril and gave it a third huge kick. The scrabbling tendrils lost their grip, and Fluffikins shot out of the greenhouse like a furry bullet, leaving behind him a long, terrified yowl that seemed to hang in the air like a sound-effect in a comic strip.

On the floor of the greenhouse the dimly glowing plant jerked and rustled, its tendrils feeling their way towards Buster's feet.

Buster turned and ran, all the way back to the blue Goatfield's Garden Centre shed that stood near the kitchen door. He fumbled for the latch with shaking fingers, glad that the Hodges didn't bother locking it. Inside, just as he had hoped, were shelves and shelves of deadly-looking weedkiller. Fake Auntie Pauline hated weeds; whenever a frail green shoot appeared through her precious gravel she would immediately drench the whole area in chemicals with names like WEED-B-GONE and DIE, BUTTERCUP, DIE! Buster selected a particularly nasty-looking can called GOATFIELD'S WEED DOOM and pulled on an outsize pair of rubber gloves. He knew Mum wouldn't approve of him using weedkillers, but there were times when dangerous chemicals came in handy, and this was definitely one of them. He scurried back to the greenhouse.

Pablo the plant was lying on the floor where Buster had left it, glowing slightly, its tendrils still twining to and fro.

Stepping as close to it as he dared, Buster up-ended the can of weedkiller and turned his face away, trying not to breathe the fumes as the noxious fluid came gurgling out. He soaked the plant's leaves, he soaked its lashing tendrils, he poured Weed Doom into its roots and the open, shrilling mouth. Then, when the green light had faded and the movements of the tendrils had grown faint and weak, he went back outside and closed the greenhouse door.

But as he crept back to the shed with the gloves and the empty bottle, he couldn't help noticing the green glimmer of other plants, growing and glowing in cold frames and glass-houses and plastic tunnels in other people's gardens. *Where do they come from?* he thought, letting himself back into the silent house. They didn't feel like anything that belonged in Smogley. They didn't feel like anything that belonged on earth at all.

He looked up at the night sky, which seem suddenly huge and cold and full of stars. Was that where Pablo and his friends had come from? Had they drifted here from some far-off plant planet, their seeds blowing like thistledown on the solar wind?

They can't have! Hurrying back to his room, he snuggled down deep under the duvet, trying to forget the idea. But it took him a long time to get back to sleep, and when he did he dreamed that he was playing football against a team of ravening Space Sprouts, and they were winning 37-nil.

5
SPROUT OF CONTROL

Morning found the garden looking normal and harmless, and as he showered and dressed Buster tried to convince himself that the battle in the greenhouse had been nothing but a bad dream. But as he went down the stairs he could already hear Fake Auntie Pauline's shrill, indignant voice.

"Someone has tried to murder Pablo!" she declared, turning to Buster as he came into the kitchen. "He's lying on the greenhouse floor with his poor pot smashed to smithereens!"

Buster poured himself a bowl of muesli and sat down between Polly and Fake Uncle Tim, trying not to look too guilty. "Bad luck, Auntie Pauline," he said. "Still, you can always get another plant to replace him. What about a nice geranium this time?"

"Replace Pablo?" Fake Auntie Pauline couldn't have looked more horrified if Buster had picked his nose at table, or said "afters" instead of "dessert". "I said somebody had *tried* to murder him. I didn't say they'd succeeded! Pablo is still very much alive. Come and see!"

They all trooped after her down to the greenhouse, and what they saw there made Buster's heart sink into his socks.

Pablo the plant had not just survived the weed-killer attack — he seemed to have thrived on it. The ugly ball of leaves and tendrils almost filled the greenhouse now, and poking out of the stem were six or seven strange little sticky warts. Fake Auntie Pauline gave a cry of joy when when she saw them. "Those weren't there earlier! They must have sprouted while we were having breakfast! They're buds! My clever little Pablo is going to have babies!"

* * *

"It was you, wasn't it?" asked Polly, when Fake Uncle Tim dropped them off at school on his way to work later. (Fake Auntie Pauline had been too excited to drive — when they last saw her, she had

48

been talking about rushing down to Goatfield's Garden Centre to ask Gordon Goatfield's advice and buy an even bigger pot for Pablo.)

"Yes," admitted Buster. "Well, you can't blame me. There's something wrong with those plants. You've seen what they do to people. And. . ." He hesitated, wondering if he ought to tell her the whole story. Fake Cousin Polly was one of those people who thought there had to be a perfectly logical explanation for everything, and he wasn't sure if she'd believe his story of the glowing, hissing, singing Space-Sprout that had attacked him and Fluffikins last night. But it was her mum's greenhouse, after all, and he thought she deserved to know, so he took a deep breath and told her everything.

When he had finished, Polly sat down on her tuba case and looked thoughtful. "I'm sure there must be a perfectly logical explanation for this," she said.

"I knew you'd say that! We've got to do something!"

"Are you sure you weren't dreaming?"

"Of course I'm sure!"

"But plants don't . . . I mean, they don't *move*. . ."

"Yes, they do," said Buster. "It's just that usually

they move really slowly. They stick a root out here and a tendril there, like a runner bean climbing up a trellis. These new ones move faster, that's all. . . And you said yourself there are some kinds of plant that eat flies and insects and stuff. . ."

"Yes, but not *cats*," Polly protested. "I can't believe a plant would try and eat dear little Fluffikins. . ."

"Well, have you seen him today?" asked Buster.

"Yes," admitted Polly. "He was hiding in the back of the hall cupboard, looking all strange and shivery. And he wouldn't touch his Kittysnax. . ."

"Well, there you are then!" Buster said. "And what about all those other cats that have gone missing? And that lady who lost her budgie? I bet she'd left one of those new plants near the cage, and as soon as it got dark, *voom*. Feathers and all."

"But you don't have any proof, do you?" Polly insisted, still hoping that Buster was wrong. "I mean, you can't prove any of it, can you?"

Buster pulled up the leg of his trousers, hoping that there would be a mark where Pablo's tentacles had wrapped round him. There wasn't.

"I still think you were dreaming," said Polly. "Now, give me a hand with my tuba. . ."

"I thought school orchestra practice was on

Mondays," Buster grumbled, lugging the enormous black case up the school steps.

"It is," said Polly proudly. "But Miss Taylor wants me to play it for her this afternoon. . ."

* * *

That day was even weirder than the day before, which had been pretty weird itself. Miss Ellis had picked up a whole car-load of mixed plants from Goatfield's on her way in: vegetables, bedding plants, marigolds, sunflowers – and, of course, a few trays of space-sprout seedlings. The school garden wasn't ready for planting yet, but the seedlings were all being potted up and kept on classroom window sills. Buster steered well clear of the sprouts, but by morning break half his class seemed to have fallen for the rubbery little things. "Miss, Miss, Missss," people kept asking, "can this one be *mine*? I want to take care of *this* one. . ." Everybody was smiling, but in a creepy, sleepy way, as if their minds were somewhere else entirely. When Buster handed in his scribble-covered geography worksheet Miss Ellis gave it a gold star without even looking at it. And as for Mr Jaffajee. . .

"I wish I'd never given him that stupid sprout!" wailed Polly, coming to find Buster in the playground that lunchtime. "He's got it in his office, and he keeps singing to it!"

"What does he sing?" asked Buster.

"The theme from *Titanic* and a selection of Songs from the Shows," said Polly, blushing with embarrassment for her favourite teacher. "Everybody's laughing at him. At least, everybody who isn't too busy thinking about their own plants. . ."

Buster looked around the playground. There were no footie matches going on, no fights, no games of war or tag or kiss-chase, and even Masher Harris, the school bully, was wandering about with a dazed grin, dreaming of organic compost and decorative flowerpots.

"I think these new plants are like cuckoos," Buster said. "As soon as they open they squirt this polleny stuff at the person who's nearest, and then that person has to look after them, the way a mother bird has to look after a cuckoo in her nest, even though it isn't hers. Once you've been got, they don't look like ugly little sprouts any more; they look like lovely orchids with all colourful petals and stuff. . . Once you've been got, your plant becomes the most important thing in the world. You heard the way your mum called you Pablo yesterday? I bet she cares more about that sprout now than she does about you. . ."

"Gordon Goatfield would never sell plants if they were dangerous. . ." said Polly, who was looking as if she might burst into tears at any moment.

"Maybe they've got him too," said Buster.

"But where do they come from?"

"Up there," Buster told her, pointing.

"The school clock tower?"

"No, outer space! Don't you see? They're alien space-sprouts, and they're here to take over!"

"Things don't really come from outer space, do they?" asked Polly nervously. "I mean, only in films. . ."

"Those cabbages do," said Buster. He hadn't been sure until now, but as soon as he said it he knew it was true. "And how long do you think they'll be satisfied with raw meat and the odd stray cat? How long before they start eating *people*?"

Polly gulped. "What can we do? Should we go to the police?"

"They'd never believe us," said Buster grimly. "When me and Tundi rang up to tell them there were dinosaurs loose in the park they just laughed and put the phone down."

"But there weren't dinosaurs loose in the park."

"No, but the principle's the same. Policemen are grown-ups, so they haven't got any imaginations, so they'd never believe in man-eating space-sprouts. Anyway, I bet the sprouts have got them too. Alien invaders always take over the policemen first, I've seen it on telly. We've got to investigate, find out how many of these things there are. Come on."

With Polly trailing behind him he hurried through the eerie silence of the playground to the school gate. Miss Taylor was supposed to be on playground-duty, but she was just staring blankly into space with a mild smile. When she saw Polly she roused herself just enough to say, "You'll be sure to come to the music-room after school today, won't you?"

"Yes, Miss Taylor," promised Polly. "I haven't forgotten."

"Good girl," said the music teacher. "I've composed a little piece of music to play to my pet plant, Ludwig, and there's a lovely tuba part. . ." The dreamy smile slid back across her face like a curtain closing, and she paid no attention at all as Buster slipped out through the school gates.

"Buster!" hissed Polly, stopping at the gate and

staring after him in horror. "Where are you going?"

"To Goatfield's Garden Centre," said Buster. "That's where these sprout things come from, isn't it?"

"But you *know* we aren't supposed to leave the playground!"

"Do you want to find out about the sprouts or not?" asked Buster.

"Well, yes, but afternoon lessons start in five minutes. . ." Polly gingerly stuck a toe out on to the pavement, then quickly pulled it back as if she had been burnt.

Buster was getting impatient. "Oh, come on, Podge," he said. "Even brainboxes like you are allowed a day off when the whole town's being taken over by evil cat-eating veg. . ."

Too late, he realized that he had used her cruel nickname. Polly glared at him and her face turned first white, then red, then an interesting shade of purple. "This is all a joke, isn't it!" she said. "All these space-sprouts and cosmic cabbages! There's nothing going on at all, really! Just because people develop an interest in gardening doesn't mean their brains have been taken over! You've just been winding me up, so you can have a laugh at stupid old Podge!" She

stepped back into the playground and slammed the gate shut.

"But Podge – I mean, Polly. . .!" Buster shouted, as she stalked back into the playground.

"You can play your silly games without me!" Polly shouted over her shoulder. For a moment she really did feel sure that it was all one of Buster's stupid jokes, and it wasn't until she caught another glimpse of Miss Taylor's dreamy smile that she started to doubt it. But by then it was too late to follow Buster: he was already hurrying away down Crisp Street heading for the bus stop on Dancers Road.

"Single to Goatfield's Garden Centre, please," he told the driver of the 36a.

"Ah!" beamed the driver, looking up from the ugly little sprout which squatted in a pot on his dashboard. "Goatfield's, eh! You'll be wanting one of these lovely new orchids!"

6
THE BIG GARDEN CENTRE OF HORRORS

Until a few months ago, the low-lying land on the west side of the town, between the new housing estate and the Smogley-to-Bunchester canal, had been marshy wasteground, home to wild birds and rare plants. People had gone there to walk their dogs, children had made secret camps among the thorn bushes, and there had been talk of turning it into a nature reserve. Then Smogley Town Council decided to let Gordon Goatfield concrete over the whole area and build his garden centre. "After all," said the councillors, as they shared out the hefty bribe that Gordon Goatfield had paid them, "who needs nature when they've got a lovely garden?"

The garden centre was an enormous square blue building with a sort of spire at one end. As Buster made his way towards it through a maze of greenhouses and gro-bags, piles of paving-slabs and enormous open-air displays of garden plants, he thought it looked like a cathedral made out of lego.

Inside, the loudspeakers were playing a synthesized version of *In an English Country Garden* and hundreds of customers were tramping to and fro, pushing shopping trolleys full of conifer seedlings and bags of bulbs. There was no sign of any space-sprouts, but many of the shoppers had the dim, mindless smiles of people in TV commercials, and Buster guessed that they were thinking about the alien plants already growing in their greenhouses. The staff were all smiling too, shambling about in their blue Goatfield's Garden Centre dungarees like an army of unusually cheerful zombies.

Buster hurried past rows of shiny lawnmowers, zigzagged between ye tables of *Ye Olde Englishe Coffee & Pretzel Shoppe* and arrived breathless and nervous at the Information Desk. The lady behind the counter turned her smile on Buster. "And what can we do for you, little boy?"

Buster realized he didn't really know what he

was going to ask her. Her glassy-eyed grin told him that she'd already been sproutified, so there was no point trying to find out the truth about the plants from her. He gave her his politest smile. "I'd like to see Gordon Goatfield, please," he announced.

"I'm sorry, dear," said the lady, still smiling. "Mr Goatfield is very, very busy."

"But I've got a serious complaint," he tried.

"A complaint?" asked the lady.

"Yes. It's these sprout things you've been handing out—"

"You mean our luscious new orchids?" The information lady's smile grew even smilier. "You know, *I* thought they looked like sprouts at first. Then I took a closer look and I saw how beautiful they really are; all those wonderful colours, beautiful petals—"

"They haven't got any petals!" shouted Buster, losing patience. "They just make you think they have! They do something to your brain! They're evil!"

To his surprise, she didn't tell him to clear off. She didn't even stop smiling. Instead she leaned closer to the little microphone on the counter and Buster heard her amplified voice booming out of every loudspeaker in the centre. "Mr

Goatfield to the information desk, please! Mr Goatfield!"

"Now then!" said a cheery voice from somewhere behind Buster's right shoulder. Buster turned round, and found himself face to face with Smogley's own Gardening Guru. (Well, actually, he found himself face-to-dungaree-pocket: Gordon Goatfield was a bit taller than him.) He looked down at a king-sized pair of blue welly boots, then up at two round red cheeks like ripe tomatoes, twinkly black eyes and a mop of hair that didn't quite cover Gordon Goatfield's shiny bald head. Earphones were clamped over the Gardening Guru's cauliflower ears, with a flex leading to a walkman on his belt. Smiling down at Buster, he turned the walkman off and said, "What seems to be the trouble?"

Buster was startled. Gordon Goatfield was grinning his trademark cheesy grin, but you could tell at a glance that he wasn't in the power of the alien plants. So why was he handing them out to half of Smogley? Perhaps he didn't *know* what they were doing to people?

Buster took a deep breath. "I've got to talk to you! It's about these sprouts. . ."

"Ah!" beamed Gordon Goatfield. "You mean, *Orchidensis Goatfieldius*! You see, Sandra," he said to the smily lady, "even kids are caught up in the new plant craze. So what's the problem, sonny? Having trouble getting your orchid to grow?'

"They aren't orchids," said Buster. "That's the trouble. I don't think they're even plants, not in the usual way. And I haven't got one. But I've seen what happens to people who have. They get taken over! They've got all my teachers and my Fake Auntie and my mates Ben and Tundi! They've even brainwashed Masher Harris, and his brain's the only bit of him that *doesn't* need washing! And your weedkiller doesn't kill them, it just makes them grow bigger. . ."

Gordon Goatfield's rosy cheeks sagged as his grin faded. He stared at Buster. "You're sure?"

"I think they want to take over all of Smogley!" Buster explained.

"We should talk about this in my office," decided Gordon Goatfield, and led Buster across to a door on the far side of the indoor plants department. Inside there was a desk, two chairs, and a lot of framed pictures of Gordon Goatfield.

The Gardening Guru took off his walkman and perched on the edge of his desk. "I like a bit of music while I'm wandering around the centre," he explained. "Now, take a seat, young Buster."

Buster sank gratefully into one of the squashy swivel chairs, amazed that a grown-up was taking him seriously for once.

Gordon Goatfield seemed genuinely concerned by what Buster had told him. "I've noticed something strange about these new plants myself," he said. "They seem to have an amazing effect on people. Folks who never had any interest in gardening at all are suddenly rushing in and buying greenhouses, fertilizer, potting-compost. . ."

"My fake auntie says you were the first to find one of them," Buster told him.

"Maybe not the first," Gordon Goatfield replied, "but certainly the first to recognize them for what they are – a whole new species. I came across a seedling just before I started building the garden centre. It was growing in the marshland, not far from here. A sad little half-dead thing it was, so I took it home and started growing it in my greenhouse, just to see what happened."

"Didn't it try to squirt you with stuff?" asked Buster.

"Not that I remember," replied Gordon Goatfield.

"But that's how they get you to look after them," explained Buster, puzzled. "They make you think they look like a beautiful orchid, instead of a dirty big sprout."

"They may look like sprouts to you, Buster," beamed Gordon Goatfield, "but to us gardeners, all plants are fascinating. That's why I thought the members of my Gardening Club might like to try growing some too."

"But—"

Gordon Goatfield hushed him. "If you're right, and these plants are really affecting people's minds, we'll have to do something. . . But before we alert the authorities, there's something I'd like you to look at. Wait here. . ."

He jumped down off the desk and went out through a small door behind the desk, a door marked "Boiler Room". A blast of dry heat came out as he opened it, fluttering the piles of paper on his desk. Buster helpfully weighted them down with Mr Goatfield's walkman to stop them blowing away, and as he did so he noticed something strange. On the far side of the room, almost hidden by the desk, was a big zinc tub with earth in it. Nothing seemed to be growing there, and when he looked closer he saw that the compost in the tub had been disturbed, as if something had just been dug out of it. . .

Then Gordon Goatfield was back, carrying

something. "Have a look at this, Buster," he said kindly. "It might help you to understand. . ."

Nestling in the gardener's hands, tendrils curled around his stubby fingers, sat one of the plants. Buster scrambled backwards, knocking the chair over as he dashed for the door – but the door was locked; Gordon Goatfield must have slipped the catch down when he showed Buster in. It was a trap!

Desperately, Buster looked for another way out. There were no windows in the office, and the air-vent in the ceiling was too high for him to reach. Gordon Goatfield marched towards him, holding out the plant. Its tendrils twitched eagerly as it caught Buster's scent, and it quivered, getting ready to release its hypnotic spores. "Don't be afraid, Buster," the Gardening Guru purred. "It won't hurt you. It'll just make you see things differently. My plants need people to protect them until they are big enough to look after themselves. . ."

He thrust the plant under Buster's nose and the bud sprang open, releasing its green cloud. Just in time, Buster threw himself sideways, rolled under the desk and leaped through the Boiler Room door, slamming it shut behind him. Concrete steps led downwards, lit by a thin flickery wash of

neon. Buster ran down them without thinking, hearing the door crash open behind him and Gordon Goatfield's angry shout.

He reached the bottom, and started along a narrow corridor with sweaty concrete walls. It was hot and the light was different here: green and throbbing, and coming not from the ceiling but from somewhere ahead. . .

And then, just as he realized what the light must be and was starting to think about turning back, he came out of the corridor into a huge basement storeroom, and saw row upon row of metal tables and row upon row of the alien plants. Throbbing, pulsing, keening, they twirled their snaky tendrils, while smiling attendants in the uniforms of Goatfield's Garden Centre moved to and fro, watering the tiniest seedlings, feeding whole sides of raw meat to the car-sized monsters at the far end of the rows. Others carried watering cans, but the dark liquid they were spilling over the space-sprouts' roots wasn't water. Buster sniffed for a moment before he recognized the familiar chemical pong of Goatfield's Weed Doom. No wonder he had failed to kill Pablo! The weedkiller that Gordon Goatfield sold might be poison to earth plants, but it was tasty fertilizer for these sprouts from space!

"Stop him!" bellowed a voice somewhere behind, and Buster remembered he was in the middle of being chased and started running again. The dozy attendants noticed him at last and tried to cut him off as he dashed between the rows of tables, but they were too preoccupied with their plants to be much good at it and he ducked easily past them. The plants themselves were more of a danger; they writhed frenziedly, lashing out at him with their sticky tendrils as he passed, and twice he had to pause and wrench himself free. Luckily, Gordon Goatfield was having the same problem, and Buster was still well ahead of him when he reached another stairway on the far side of the underground storeroom and ran up it and out into the bright, normal-looking garden centre.

Shivery with fright and sick from the sweet smell of the sprouts, he scrambled into a narrow hiding place between two racks of garden gnomes as Gordon Goatfield came bursting out through the storeroom door. Almost at once, Buster realized his mistake. There was no way out, and Gordon Goatfield was making his way slowly and deliberately towards him, checking every nook and cranny where a Buster might be hidden.

Buster looked round frantically. There were not many customers in sight, and the few he could see were all obviously under the control of the plants – he could shout for help all he liked, but none of them would come to his rescue. Closer and closer came Gordon Goatfield, until Buster could hear the heavy rasp of his breath and the faint slithery squeak of his wellies on the lino. . .

. . .and then, suddenly, a trolley came careering out of a nearby aisle and skidded to a halt just in front of Buster's hiding place. "Oh, Mr Goatfield!" gushed a familiar voice. It was Fake Auntie Pauline.

"Good morning, madam," said Gordon Goatfield, trying to peer past her into the gaps between the gnome-displays.

"I need to talk to you!" twittered Fake Auntie Pauline. "Somebody has tried to attack my superb orchid. They failed, but now that poor Pablo is in bud I'm frightened that they might try again, and you did say in your newsletters that we should come straight to you if we were worried about anything. . ."

"In bud, eh?" Gordon Goatfield's eyes glittered, and he forgot Buster for a moment. "Excellent! Your plant is one of the first to mature. Soon he will need you no longer, but for the next day or so you must take extra-special care of him. . ."

As quiet as a mouse, Buster slid out of his hiding place and crept away, keeping Fake Auntie Pauline's heavily-laden trolley between himself and the Gardening Guru. He wanted to run, but he knew that would attract attention, so he attached himself to a young couple who were making their way to the check-out and tried not to look too nervous or impatient while they queued up with their trolleyful of gravel and potting compost. He was pretty sure that Gordon Goatfield would have escaped from Fake Auntie Pauline's clutches by now – but he was also pretty sure that he would still be searching for Buster behind the garden gnome display at the far end of the centre.

While the cashier started ringing up the young couple's purchases, Buster slipped past them and headed for the exit, past an enormous pinboard where people had stuck up the most boring adverts in the whole world. "For Sale," said one, "Goatfield Lawnmaster mower with grass-box – £75." "Wanted," droned another, "Fresh horse manure – will collect."

It was pure luck that made Buster's eye fall on a small, grubby, badly-typed poster somewhere near the bottom of the board. He had walked past before it really hit him, and he risked going back for a second look. If it had really said what he thought it had, it could be the answer to all his worries!

Glancing quickly over his shoulder to make sure that Gordon Goatfield and his staff were not pursuing him, Buster tore the notice off the board and ran out through the sliding doors, across the car park and away into the sprout-haunted suburbs of Smogley.

7
THE QUIRKE BROTHERS

In a telephone box at the end of Dancer's Road, Buster dialled the number printed on the poster. The phone rang for ages, and while he was waiting he had time to read the poster again.

GHOULIES? GHOSTIES?
LONG-LEGGETY BEASTIES?
THINGS GOING BUMP IN THE NIGHT?
Don't delay – call us today
QUIRKE BROTHERS
MONSTER HUNTERS
FEROCIUOS MONSTERS QUICKLY AND
CLEENLY DEALT WITH.
GHOSTS EXERCISED. ALIENS ZAPPED.
NO MESS. NO BOTHER.

VERY REASONUBBLE RATES.
QUIRKE BROS. INC. FOR ALL YOUR
MONSTER-HUNTING NEEDS.

Buster had always supposed that there must be such people as monster hunters, but this was the first time he'd actually seen an advert for any. What a stroke of luck, that he should find it just when Smogley was being menaced by Gordon Goatfield's killer veg!

A woman's voice answered the phone. She sounded tired.

"Is that Quirke Bros. Inc?" asked Buster, in his politest talking-to-grown-ups voice.

"What?" said the woman.

"I'd like to talk to the chief monster hunter, please. . ." Buster told her.

"The chief who? Are you some friend of Harvey and Cole?"

"I don't think so," Buster confessed, starting to get confused. "I just found one of their adverts and. . ."

"Adverts?" The woman on the other end of the phone gave an exasperated sigh. "I suppose this is another of their schemes. When I said they should get a weekend job I was thinking of a paper-round. . ."

"Er. . ." said Buster.

"Well, they're not here, but I suppose you could leave your number and I'll tell them to call you when they get in."

Buster couldn't remember Fake Auntie Pauline's phone number, but he gave the woman her address in Acacia Crescent and told her that that was where the Quirke Brothers could find him.

The phone call had cost him most of his money, so he had to walk all the way back into town. By the time he got there the school was deserted, except for Mr Creaber, who was sweeping the playground and paused just long enough to shout, "Oi! You! Hop it!" when he saw Buster peering through the locked gates. At least *he* hadn't been got by the veg yet, thought Buster, as he turned wearily towards Acacia Crescent. But then he remembered all the things growing in the storerooms under Goatfield's Garden Centre. Soon everyone in Smogley would be growing a space-sprout — and when the sprouts got big enough they would turn on their owners, and then. . .

And then what? What was Gordon Goatfield planning? Why was he in league with these green invaders? Was it just so that he would make more money out of his garden centre? But how did he expect to spend any of his earnings, if everybody else had been eaten by sprouts?

Buster's brain made little creaking noises as he struggled to think it all through. It just didn't make any sense. . .

By the time he reached Fake Auntie Pauline's house she was already home, her enormous car ticking and pinging on the forecourt as its engine cooled. A trail of potting compost led through the house and out across the back garden towards the greenhouse, where she was busy repotting her beloved Pablo. She must have remembered to pick up Polly on her way back from the garden centre, though, because the tuba case was blocking the hall like an upturned boat, only with silver catches and POLLY HODGE CLASS 2a written on it in tippex.

Buster squeezed past it and hurried upstairs to knock on Polly's door.

"Who is it?" said a teary-sounding voice from inside.

"Buster," said Buster. "Can I come in?"

"No," said Polly. "Go away." And he heard the unmistakable sound of a bookcase being pushed against the other side of the door.

"Don't mind her, Buster," said Fake Uncle Tim,

coming out of the bathroom to find Buster standing disconsolately on the landing in front of Polly's door. "She's in a bit of a bad mood. I don't think her tuba thing went very well this afternoon. Miss Taylor told her off, or something. . ."

Oh yeah, sure, thought Buster: everybody knew that Polly *never* got told off. Of course, he couldn't tell Fake Uncle Tim the real reason why the girl was upset; because Buster had called her Podge, and she had thought he was making fun of her. He stomped downstairs, feeling horrible. Polly was all right; it wasn't her fault she was a bit fat, and he really hadn't meant to upset her. Now he had nobody to help him in the fight against the plants from outer space.

Wondering what to do, he checked Fake Uncle Tim's computer, and found another cheery e-mail from Mum. This one came with two photographs; one of a lot of mud-splattered lollipop ladies scrambling over an assault course with an arrow pointing to one labelled ME!! and one of a skydiving Mum clutching her lollipop for dear life as she jumped out of a big aeroplane. For a moment Buster seriously considered telling her everything that was going on in Smogley, but then he changed his mind; if the photos were anything to go by she already had enough to worry about at Camp Kludge. He typed her a chirpy, nothingy sort of reply instead, and went off to see if there was anything to eat.

The kitchen was a disaster area. Fake Auntie Pauline had announced that she was too busy in the greenhouse to bother cooking, so Fake Uncle Tim was attempting to make the evening meal on his own. "How am I supposed to get these sausages in the toaster?" he complained as Buster wandered in.

"Uncle Tim," Buster asked, prising the mangled sausages free and shoving them under the grill where they belonged, "have you noticed anything strange about Auntie Pauline lately?"

"Strange?" Fake Uncle Tim looked out of the kitchen window as his wife reeled past on the way to the greenhouse, her face and clothes smeared with potting compost, clutching a carrier bag full of raw, bloody meat in one hand and a watering can in the other. "No, not really, why?"

"It's this plant business," Buster prompted. "You don't think she's getting a bit, well, obsessed?"

"Oh, that!" Fake Uncle Tim chuckled quietly, scooping some baked beans on to a plate and putting it into the dishwasher. "Pauline's very enthusiastic; she gets a bee in her bonnet about things from time to time. Last year it was the Amateur Dramatic Society; this year it's Pablo; next year it'll be something else. Better to just ignore it, Buster. Do I mash these spuds before they're baked, or after?"

Has he been taken over too? Buster wondered, watching Fake Uncle Tim's glazed expression as he tried to mash some potatoes with an egg-whisk. But he didn't really think any alien cabbages were responsible – Fake Uncle Tim had always been like that.

Just then, the doorbell rang. Fake Uncle Tim looked up, blinking through potato-splattered spectacles. "Would you mind seeing who that is, Buster?" he asked.

Buster trotted to the door. Two boys stood on the front step. One was fair-haired and a little bit older than Buster, the other was dark, and slightly younger. They were both bending forward under the weight of enormous rucksacks, and Buster didn't have the faintest idea who they were.

"You must be Buster Bayliss," said the older one, holding out his hand for Buster to shake. Unfortunately the movement made him over-balance and he went toppling sideways into the shrubbery with a faint cry.

"Quirke Brothers," said the younger boy. "We hunt monsters. You left a message with our mum."

"He means our secretary," burbled a voice from the depths of the shrubbery.

"Oh, yeah, that's right. Our secretary," the younger Quirke corrected hastily.

Buster was not impressed. When he asked for monster hunters he had been expecting grown-ups, with armoured Land Rovers and enormous guns. "Are you *really* monster hunters?" he asked.

"Course we are," spluttered the older Quirke, standing up and pulling bits of hedge out of his hair. "I'm Harvey, and this is Cole."

"But you're just kids!" Buster objected. "Where did you learn to hunt monsters? Don't you have to go to monster-hunting school or something?"

Harvey Quirke shook his head. "Not us. We picked it up on the job, mostly. Studied at the Middle School of Life."

"And the Kindergarten of Hard Knocks," explained his brother.

"So what monsters have you caught?" asked Buster.

"Oh, just the usual, you know. . ." said Harvey Quirke modestly. "A few vampires. The odd slime-creature. Orcs. Demons. Goblins. A werewolf or two."

"Last week Lawrence called us in to exercise this really scary ghost in his back garden. . ." said Cole.

"Lawrence is the boy who lives next door," explained Harvey. "And you mean 'exorcise'," he reminded his brother.

"But it turned out to be just a nightie that his Mum had left out on the washing line," Cole went on.

"Shhhh! Don't tell Mr Bayliss that!" his brother hissed, nudging him, and they both toppled over and lay on their backs, pinned down by the weight of their rucksacks.

Buster glanced back down the hall to the kitchen. Black smoke was spilling out from under the door, bringing with it a smell of burnt sausage and feeble cries of "Oh, bother! Er. . . Buster? Polly?"

He stepped out into the front garden, pulling the door shut behind him, and helped the Quirke Brothers to their feet. They seemed a bit young, but he had to do *something*, and at the moment they were the only allies he had. And maybe they really were monster hunters. Harvey's talk of goblins and vampires sounded pretty impressive.

"How much do you charge for killing a rampaging space-sprout?" he asked. "There are loads of them, trying to take over Smogley. They're strong and fierce and intelligent, and they take over people's brains and make them their slaves."

"Cool!" said the Quirke Brothers.

"I want to start with the one in the greenhouse," Buster told them.

"Is it a man-eater?" asked Harvey, in a businesslike way.

"Not exactly," admitted Buster. "At least, not yet. It'd definitely be a cat-eater if you gave it half a chance. . ."

"Let's see," mused Harvey, pulling a handwritten price list out of his pocket. "For disposing of your basic cat-eating plant . . . that'd be £100."

"£100?" Buster felt about in his pockets. "I've got 35p and some chewing gum."

"That'll do," said Harvey quickly, taking it from him. "Now, where's this monster?"

Buster led them to the end of Acacia Crescent, then doubled back up the narrow alleyway that stretched along the backs of the gardens, littered with broken bikes and other things the dustmen were too picky to remove. A whole kitchen sink that someone had turfed out perched like an unlikely bird on its nest of pipes and taps, and gave off a deep, echoey *bong* when Buster tripped over it. In the gathering twilight, deep pools of shadow lay between the bramble-patches and dustbins in the alleyway, so it took quite some time for the boys to creep along, especially since the Quirke Brothers' huge rucksacks kept getting hooked up on briars. "What's in them, anyway?" asked Buster.

"Vital equipment," replied Harvey Quirke mysteriously.

At last they came to the fence that marked the end of Fake Auntie Pauline's garden, and all stood on tiptoe to peer over. There was the greenhouse, crouching against the metal blade of the shark-fin sculpture, glowing with a dim, green light. Buster could see Fake Auntie Pauline moving about inside, but the glass had steamed up so that it was hard to make out Pablo. He pointed. "It's in there. . ."

"Looks nasty!" said Harvey.

"No, not that, that's my Fake Auntie Pauline. . ."

"A fake auntie, eh?" The monster hunter narrowed his eyes. "You mean the plants have done away with your real auntie and she's a replica, in the power of an alien overlord?'

"No, no, no. . ." Buster was finding it difficult to explain all this in whispers. "She's always been a fake auntie; I don't have any real aunties."

"So the replica must be a fake fake auntie?" asked Cole, frowning.

"There aren't any replicas," hissed Buster. "There's just a sprouty-cabbagy alien in that shed that's taken control of my fake auntie's brain somehow and it's making her look after it. I want to destroy it, but it's big and it's dangerous and it laps up Gordon Goatfield's weedkiller and asks for more. So what are you going to do about it?"

Harvey and Cole set down their packs and rummaged around inside them, turfing out shoeboxes with crayoned signs on the lids that said things like "Vampire-killing Kit" and "Spare silver bullits". When they finally straightened up they were each holding one of the biggest water pistols that Buster had ever seen.

"Two hundred litre Squirtmaster Gloosh-o-matics," said Harvey proudly. "These babies will knock an Action Man off the top of a flowerpot from six hundred paces."

"Most people have to do that by hand," Cole added.

"Your killer sprout'll be laughing on the other

side of its face when it gets a burst from one of these between its eyes," Harvey said, filling his weapon from an old lemonade bottle, then passing the bottle to Cole.

"But they're water pistols!" protested Buster, starting to panic. "And plants *like* water!" There were just three thoughts in his mind as he watched the intrepid monster hunters pumping up their plastic arsenal.

1: *They're total muppets!*
2: *Pablo the Plant is going to eat them for tea,*
   I mean dinner!
3: *And it's all my fault!*

Just then they heard the greenhouse door slide open. They all ducked down, squinting through cracks in the fence. Fake Auntie Pauline wandered out of the greenhouse and carefully shut the door behind her before weaving her way unsteadily towards the house, drawn by the smells of burnt sausage and freshly washed beans that were starting to drift across the twilit garden.

"Now's our chance!" hissed Harvey Quirke. Buster looked round. Both Quirke Brothers had strapped torches to their heads. Now, at a word from Harvey, they switched them on, dazzling

Buster. Cole pulled a dustbin into position and both brothers scrambled up on to it and over the fence, dropping heavily down on to the gravel on the far side.

"No!" pleaded Buster, imagining how big Pablo would be when it had eaten the two monster hunters. But the Quirke Brothers ignored him. There was nothing for it but to go after them.

By the time he caught up with them they were crouching outside the greenhouse door, Gloosh-o-matics at the ready. Harvey reached for the door handle, nodding to his brother. "Fifty-litre bursts, maximum squirt. . ."

He hauled the door open and the beams from their head-torches sliced through the thick, misty air inside. For a moment they saw nothing but shadows and swirling water droplets; then, at the far end of the greenhouse, something moved.

Pablo was huge now; as big as the biggest of the plants that Buster had seen in the storeroom under Goatfield's Garden Centre. He reared from his pot, leaning towards the three terrified boys, and the opening between his thick leaves gaped, letting out a horrible, unearthly hiss. The wet air of the greenhouse was suddenly full of tendrils, stretching towards the door like a hundred snakes.

"AAAAAAAAAAAAAAAAAAAAAAAAAAAARGH!" said Buster, Harvey and Cole, and both monster hunters squeezed the triggers of their Gloosh-o-matics. For a moment the twin jets of water actually forced the furious sprout backwards, just long enough for Buster to slam the door shut, trapping a couple of its writhing tentacles. Another second and all three boys were crouching behind Seamus O'Hooligan's stainless steel sculpture and shivering like jellies.

"It was a mon . . . a mon . . . a mon . . . a mon . . . a mon . . . a MONSTER!" stuttered Harvey.

"I don't like this game!" whimpered Cole.

"But you've seen things like that before, haven't you?" Buster asked. "I mean, all those vampires and orcs and trolls and things that you said you'd dealt with. . ."

Harvey Quirke turned a pale, scared face towards him. "They were mainly in computer games," he admitted. "In fact, now I come to think of it, they were *all* in computer games."

"Our mum kept nagging us to get a weekend job," explained Cole. "So we put up those adverts saying we were monster hunters. We didn't think anybody would *actually want us to actually hunt an actual monster*. We thought you were just playing a game. I want to go home!"

"That was one of those new orchids, wasn't it?" whispered Harvey. "My teacher's got one of them. Do you think his is going to turn into something like that?"

Gingerly, they all peered over the edge of the sculpture. The tentacles that had been severed when Buster closed the door lay on the path outside, still wriggling feebly. The greenhouse itself was silent, but the green glow throbbed inside, and Buster could sense Pablo in there, scenting the air, feeling for the three hot, tasty bodies that had just escaped him, gathering his strength, getting ready to—

The greenhouse exploded. Shards and angles of glass whirled upwards, filling the twilight with hurtling reflections. The metal frame sagged, and Pablo the Plant hauled himself out through the wreckage, dragging himself along by his roots and tentacles, heaving towards the place where Buster and the others crouched.

"AAAAAAAAAAAAAAAAAAAAAAAAAAARGH!" they all said again.

Two seconds later, when Fake Auntie Pauline came rushing out of the kitchen door to see what all the noise was, Buster, Harvey and Cole were

huddled together on the roof of the shed, looking down at her.

"Pablo?" she asked. She stared worriedly towards the far end of the garden, not noticing the boys. The space-sprout was a green, throbbing blob, hauling itself slowly towards the house.

"Good grief!" shouted Fake Uncle Tim, stepping out on to the patio. "What's *that*?" He took a few paces towards the lurching plant, then jumped back as a tendril lashed at him. "Is this your plant, dear? Something's gone wrong with it! It's . . . *moving*!"

"It's just hungry," snapped Fake Auntie Pauline. "Nothing to be afraid of! Gordon warned me that this might happen as the plant matures. I'd better get down to the supermarket and pick up some more meat. . ."

"Meat?" Fake Uncle Tim hurried back to the safety of the doorstep. "You mean that thing's carnivorous? Then we've got to get rid of it! Call the police or the army or *Gardeners' Question Time*! How many more of them are there?"

"Don't be silly, Timothy." Fake Auntie Pauline strode fearlessly down the garden, and Pablo's tentacles shivered into stillness; he recognized her scent, and however hungry he was he knew that she was his protector, and he could not eat her . . . yet. She knelt down, stroking the rubbery leaves, and Pablo gave a soft, high-pitched purr. Then Fake Auntie Pauline gently plucked something from the stem of the plant and walked back up the garden, holding it out for her husband to see.

It was a tiny new sprout, freshly budded.

"No!" shouted Buster, startling both Quirke Brothers so much that they nearly dropped off the shed roof. "Fake Uncle Tim! *Don't sniff that sprout!*"

But it was too late. Fake Auntie Pauline shoved the alien plant under her husband's nose, and the sudden puff of green was clearly visible for a moment in the light from the kitchen doorway. As the contented smile spread slowly across her husband's face, Fake Auntie Pauline turned towards the shed. Fake Uncle Tim might not have heard Buster's shout of warning, but she had.

"You!" she growled.

Buster had never thought of Fake Auntie Pauline as an athlete, but the way she grabbed a broom and used it to pole-vault up on to the shed roof would probably have qualified her for the British Olympic team. There was one of those wooden prongs called a Witches' Peak on the end of the shed, supposed to stop witches from resting there – but it didn't stop Fake Auntie Pauline. She grabbed it with both hands and heaved herself towards the terrified boys. "I don't need to go to the supermarket!" she laughed madly. "I've all the plant-food I need right here!"

8
THE QUITE-A-MESS EXPERIMENT

The Quirke Brothers were not going to let themselves be fed to Pablo without a fight. The jets from their Squirtmaster Gloosh-o-matics hit Fake Auntie Pauline full in the face, and she overbalanced and fell backwards off the roof, landing with a thud on top of Fake Uncle Tim, who had set his plant down on the kitchen window sill and come running to help her. Buster was sort of impressed, but he didn't see how even the Quirke Brothers' mean water-pistol work would help; short of jumping down and joining Pablo and the possessed grown-ups, there was no way off the roof.

Then he heard the nicest sound he had ever heard in his life. It was the sound of a window opening just above him, and Fake Cousin Polly's voice saying, "Buster! All of you! Up here! Quick!"

Polly's bedroom window sill was only a about a metre above the level of the shed roof, and the Quirke Brothers threw their water pistols up to her and then let her help them up to safety. Buster followed. Behind him he could hear Fake Auntie Pauline's scrabbling attempts to climb back on to the shed, and then Fake Uncle Tim shouting, "Pauline! They're going into the house! We'll trap them there!"

Groaning, Polly dragged Buster over her windowsill and into her room. The Quirke Brothers were waiting near the door, looking slightly embarrassed by all the pictures of ponies and handsome boy-bands which were staring down at them from the walls. "We've got to move fast," Polly told them. "I saw everything from the window. Daddy's on the plant's side now, like Mummy. We'll have to get out of the house before they can cut us off at the front door. Follow me!"

She kicked the door open, one of the Quirke Brothers' water-pistols in either hand. The landing and the staircase were deserted, but as the frightened children reached the bottom of the stairs the kitchen door burst open, and Fake Auntie Pauline came running towards them down the hall, dripping and furious and brandishing a cake-slice. Polly sprayed her with the water pistols, and when that didn't work she sprayed the floor. Fake Auntie Pauline's old gardening slippers lost their grip on the wet parquet and down she went. Fake Uncle Tim came charging out of the kitchen just in time to trip over her and knock her down again as she struggled to her feet.

Polly hurled the empty water pistols aside and flung the front door open. "Bring my tuba!" she shouted.

The boys looked at her in amazement. "We're running from man-eating plants, Polly!" Buster shouted. "We don't need a brass section!"

"Yes, we do!" screamed Polly, already halfway down the drive. "I'll explain later!"

The Quirke Brothers grabbed the enormous black instrument case and struggled out into the night. Buster glanced back once at the writhing tangle of fake relatives in the kitchen doorway, then sprinted after the others.

In the front garden he came to a halt. He had to. Polly and the Quirkes had stopped halfway down the drive and were retreating slowly towards the house. Buster almost crashed into them as they backed towards him.

"What's wrong?" he asked.

Then he saw.

All along Acacia Crescent, people were emerging from front doors and garden gates. Dads in their carpet slippers, mums still clutching cups of tea, children in pyjamas and dressing gowns; dozens of Fake Auntie Pauline's neighbours were converging on her house, and from their bland smiles and the way the street lamps glittered in their glassy eyes, Buster could tell that they were all in the power of the alien veg!

There was no escape. Pablo must have whistled and hooted the news of the Quirke Brothers' attack to every other plant in Acacia Crescent, and now they were sending out their slaves to stop Buster and his friends from getting away.

They turned back to the house, but there were Fake Auntie Pauline and Fake Uncle Tim in the front porch, and squeezing between them, tendrils coiling, was Pablo. "Din-dins, Pablo, dear!" said Fake Auntie Pauline, and the dark maw between his leaves gaped black as he reached for Buster, who was nearest.

Polly fumbled with the catches on her tuba case.

"Oh, help!" squeaked Harvey Quirke.

"Mum's always going on at us to eat our greens," whimpered his brother. "Now greens are going to eat us!"

Buster had a last frantic look round, hoping that there was some way out. There wasn't. Pablo's tentacles brushed his face, sweet and sticky. One curled around his legs, another slithered around his elbow. He felt himself lifted off the ground, and caught the hot vegetable smell of the space-sprout's gaping mouth. . .

And then he was nearly deafened by an amazing blast of noise.

BRRRRRRAAAAAAAAP!

Buster opened his eyes. He was in mid-air, hanging by a dozen quivering tentacles over Pablo's open mouth, but the evil sprout seemed to have suddenly lost interest in eating him. It was quivering, flapping its leaves, letting out a thin shrill of alarm that could barely be heard in the surf of sound breaking over Acacia Crescent.

BRRRRROOOOOOOOOP!

Fake Auntie Pauline and Fake Uncle Tim dropped to their knees, covering their ears and writhing as if in pain. Out in the street, their

neighbours stumbled uncertainly away from the noise. The Quirke Brothers just sat staring in amazement at Polly, who was blowing with all her might into the mouthpiece of her tuba.

BRUUUUUUUUUUPfffffff...

Pablo gave a last bat-like squeal and exploded, splattering greenish goo all up the freshly-decorated front of Fake Auntie Pauline's house. Polly had stopped blowing; she was red in the face and gasping for breath, but the echoes of that final toot went rolling off along Acacia Crescent, and in greenhouses and window boxes and conservatories all along the street plants blew up, or wilted, or dropped out of their pots and lay still.

"It's dead!" whispered Harvey, staring at what was left of Pablo the plant.

"What happened?" asked Cole.

"It was the sound," puffed Polly, carefully putting her tuba back in its case. She was still gasping for breath. "I guessed it would work, but I wasn't sure. . . Poor Pablo. I never thought I'd use my tuba to kill. . ."

Buster just stared at her. He had no idea how she had known what to do, but he was very impressed.

The neighbours, who had all crumpled to the ground, stood up slowly, looking as if they weren't quite sure why they were all standing in the street together at this time of night, without their shoes or coats on. Carefully ignoring each other, they started making their way back to their own houses, all politely pretending that nothing had happened.

Fake Auntie Pauline and Fake Uncle Tim stood up too, and blinked in horrified surprise at the mess on the front of their house.

"What's that?" asked Fake Uncle Tim.

"Buster?" said Fake Auntie Pauline menacingly. "Is this one of your practical jokes?"

Buster scrambled up off the lawn where Pablo had dropped him, covered in smelly grey sludge and feeling a bit shaky. "It's all right, Fake Auntie Pauline," he said. "Come back indoors. We can explain everything. . ."

9
THE INTREPID SPROUT-HUNTERS

It wasn't easy to make Buster's fake auntie and uncle understand what had been happening to them. Fake Uncle Tim had no memory of anything that had happened after he finished ruining the dinner. "What were we doing in the front garden?" he kept asking. "What's that stuff all over the house?" Fake Auntie Pauline was even worse. She was like somebody emerging from a strange vegetable-related dream. All she remembered of the last few days was a weird little squeaky voice in her head that seemed to have been telling her what to do, and even that memory soon faded. She didn't believe a word of what Polly and Buster and their new friends were trying to tell her. "A sprout? What sprout? I don't grow vegetables, Buster; I've got a garden, not an allotment. . . The neighbours too? Aliens? Don't be ridiculous! Things like that don't happen in Acacia Crescent!"

"Absolutely not," agreed Fake Uncle Tim, and yawned cavernously. It must have been tiring being a mindless slave, because Fake Auntie Pauline started yawning too, and in a few more seconds they were both fast asleep, heads on the kitchen table, snoring.

"They don't remember a thing!" said Polly. "I was planning to go to the police, but what's the point? Even if I kill their plants they won't believe me, and then they'll just fall asleep."

Buster turned from the sink, where he had been washing the exploded-space-sprout goo out of his hair. "There's one thing I don't understand," he said. (Actually there were a lot of things Buster didn't understand, like algebra and French and what grown-ups see in sunbathing, but this was the one that was on his mind at that particular moment.) "How did you know that your tuba would make Pablo go off bang?"

Polly looked pleased with herself. "I didn't, not for sure; but I had a hunch that it would work. Miss Taylor specially wanted me to bring my tuba into school today, remember? She's been veggiefied too; she had a plant called Ludwig that she keeps on top of her piano. She was potty about it, and she'd written a special piece of music which she wanted us to record so that she could play it to the plant and help it grow. She's one of those people who believe in playing music to plants. . ."

"A loony," suggested Harvey.

"Are you listening to this or not?"

"Sorry."

"Where was I? Oh yes, so we all assembled in the music room. All the best musicians from the school orchestra were there: me with my tuba, Lijian with her cello, Ian Strawbrick with his electric guitar, and Miss Taylor on the piano. She put Ludwig in the middle, where he'd be able to hear us, and we started to play.

"It went really well at first. The first bit was just cello and piano, and then Ian's guitar came in, and then there was a bit for me to play; a sort of 'Boop-be-dop-de-doop-da-doo' bit. But when I was halfway through I heard Miss Taylor give a sort of a screech and I stopped playing and looked up – and Ludwig was dead. He hadn't burst, like Pablo, but he'd turned a funny shade of grey and dropped out of his pot with all his roots in the air.

"It was awful. Miss Taylor was in a terrible state. We had to go and find Mr Creaber, and he sent her home in a taxi. . ."

"So that's why you were upset earlier!" said Buster.

"Yes. . ."

"Not because I called you Podge?"

"Shut up and listen. Of course I was upset; Miss Taylor is my second favourite teacher and I felt sorry for her. It wasn't until I thought about it later that I realized what had happened – it must have been the music that killed her plant. Not just any music, though. It didn't mind the cello, or the piano, or the guitar; it died when it heard my tuba!"

"I'm not surprised," said Buster. "I've heard you practising and it nearly killed me too. . ."

"Shut up, Buster," said Polly, chucking a spoon at him.

"But I bet you're right!" he went on. "We know the plants can hear things. The first time I was in the greenhouse with Pablo my tummy burbled, and you could tell he didn't like it; he sort of quivered. And then when I was out in the garden the other night I could hear Pablo whistling and singing. . ."

"They must use sound to communicate with

each other!" suggested Harvey Quirke. "They've probably got really delicate hearing. No wonder your tuba was too much for Pablo. . ."

"I think any brass instrument would have the same effect," said Polly modestly. "It's probably something to do with frequency and resonance. . ."

"But how does that help us?" Cole complained. "We may have made Acacia Crescent safe, but we can't go round playing the tuba in every greenhouse in Smogley! We'd be puffed out!"

"We need help," said Harvey. "We've got to form an intrepid Anti-Sprout Squad."

"The school orchestra!" said Polly. "I know where most of them live, and I bet they'd help!"

"But they're all sadsters," objected Buster.

"Yes, but sadsters with their own brass band instruments," Polly pointed out. "If we're going to do this properly we'll need horns; lots of horns!"

"Cor," whispered Cole, nudging Buster. "Your fake cousin's really *cool*!"

"Cool?" said Buster. He had never thought of Polly as cool before.

"Yeah," whispered Harvey, nudging him from the other side. "Has she got, you know, a boyfriend?"

"The garden centre!" said Buster quickly,

before they all got sidetracked. "That's where they're all coming from. Gordon Goatfield is in league with the sprouts, and until we've got rid of the ones in his basement Smogley will never be safe. But we'll have to move fast, before Gordon and his sprouty chums work out what we're doing. . ."

* * *

Ten minutes later Buster and Polly were scurrying through the town, careful to stick to side streets and twittens and the little overgrown pathways between back gardens. They had left the Quirke Brothers on guard at Acacia Crescent, and they were searching for brass-players.

Their first call was at the house of Lindsay Spratt, the school orchestra's trombonist. They threw bits of gravel at her bedroom window, then carefully mimicked the bland smiles of plant-people while they waited for her to open the door. But as soon as they saw Lindsay they could tell that she wasn't in the power of the veg, and they followed her through into the living room. "Those new plants?" she said, when Polly asked her. "No, Mum and Dad put one in my bedroom yesterday, but it died. When I finished practising my trombone and went to water it, it had gone all gooey. It's very odd; I'm usually good with plants. But I can't say I'm sorry: it was an ugly little thing, like a Brussels sprout. Mum and Dad are really keen on them though. They've got one each. That's where they are now, down in the greenhouse, even though it's the middle of the night. I think it's really weird. . ."

"You're right," agreed Buster, munching his way through the contents of the Spratts' biscuit tin. He quickly told her everything that he and Polly had learned about the sinister plants. Lindsay wasn't sure whether to believe him or not (Buster had once sneaked a whoopee cushion on to her seat in assembly and since then she had never thought him completely trustworthy). But here was Polly Hodge, the cleverest girl in the school, agreeing with everything Buster said; and here were her parents – or rather, here they weren't, because she had hardly seen them these last few days, they had been so busy running errands for their precious plants. . .

"All right," she said at last, when Buster told her his plan. "I'll help. . ."

"And if your mum or dad or anybody tries to make you sniff one of those plants," Polly warned her, "just give it a toot from your trombone."

It was the same in each house they called at.

Sanjay Bhattacharya's plant had been killed by the French horn blasts in his sound-proofed bedroom, and the rest of his family had been too obsessed with their own plants to notice. Ivor Phillips's parents had never succeeded in growing any of the alien plants at all, so loud were the blasts from his trumpet, but most of his friends had been veggiefied and he was only too eager to help put a stop to the Space Sprouts' plans. Belinda Branson, Henry Hill and James and Katie MacCallum were all eager to help, too; and the MacCallums even had a spare trombone.

It was after midnight when they all arrived back at Polly's house. Fake Auntie Pauline and Fake Uncle Tim were still snoring in the kitchen, but the Quirke Brothers had been busy. Not only had they retrieved their precious monster-hunting backpacks from the alley at the end of Pauline's garden, they had invented a musical instrument.

"We couldn't let you lot have all the fun," explained Harvey Quirke, as Buster and Polly and the magnificent brass-blowing seven trooped out on to the patio to admire his handiwork.

"It's called a Quirk-o-phone," said Cole proudly.

It was made out of some of the bits of abandoned plumbing from the alleyway: the old metal sink linked to about two metres of wiggly pipes, all packed into a shopping trolley for mobility. When Harvey blew an experimental blast it made a hollow bellowing noise like a burping brontosaurus, not quite as tuneful as Polly's tuba, but just as loud.

The Anti-Sprout Squad was as ready as it would ever be, thought Buster, nervously surveying his troops. Now it was time for somebody to take the lead, and as usual, it was going to have to be him.

"All right, men!" said Buster.

"And women," said Polly.

"All right, men and women. . ."

"We're only boys really," Ivor Phillips pointed out.

"And girls. . ." said Belinda Branson.

"All right, *people*," said Buster, "Atten-SHUN!"

The intrepid brass-players stood up straight, instruments at the ready.

"Does everybody know what they're doing?" asked Buster.

They all nodded, and Sanjay said, "Yo!"

"We can't afford to make any mistakes," Buster told them. "We must be alert and constantly vigilant; like meerkats. We—"

"Like whats?" asked Cole.

"Meerkats," explained Buster. "They're sort of animals. I've seen them on telly. They live in holes, and they're always vigilant. And alert. That's what we've got to be like. We've got to splatter every sprout in Smogley."

Belinda put her hand up. "But what about the plants' owners? Won't they be really cross and come after us?"

"I don't think so," said Polly. "If they're anything like Mummy and Daddy they'll just feel a bit confused and then fall fast asleep."

"Here's the plan," said Buster importantly. "Me, Polly, Harvey and Cole are going to tackle the ones at Goatfield's. The rest of you split up into groups and do the rest of the town. This is where Smogley's fight against the alien sprout menace begins! We'll fight them in the green-houses! We'll fight them in the front porches! We'll fight them under the cold frames! We'll never surrender!"

"Erm, Buster. . ." Polly was tugging at his sleeve.
"What?"
"They've gone."
Buster looked round. Sure enough, the Anti-Sprout Squad had scattered, and when he listened closely he could hear their bikes ticking away down Acacia Crescent, their excited voices

fading as they set off to do battle with the veggie invaders.

"Good speech though," said Cole encouragingly.

The four remaining Sprout Slayers didn't have bikes, and they would never have been able to cycle with the Quirk-o-phone anyway, so they would have to walk to Goatfield's. Luckily, Polly knew a short cut through the new estate. Harvey and Cole refilled their water pistols and put fresh batteries in their head-torches. Polly checked that her parents were still sleeping soundly. Buster ate some more biscuits, hoping that they would squash the flock of butterflies that seemed to be practising aerobatics in his tummy.

Then, carrying the tuba and the MacCallums' second-best trombone, pushing the Quirk-o-phone ahead of them in the squeaky-wheeled shopping trolley, they set off. This was war!

10
NIGHT OF THE LIVING VEG

In the streets and gardens of Smogley, something peculiar was happening. Again and again that night the same scene was repeated, all across the town: small figures scurrying across a back alley, or swarming over a garden fence towards a greenhouse or conservatory which throbbed dimly green. Then something caught the light; the round mouth of a trumpet or French horn poking out of a hedge, a trombone pushed carefully through a cat-flap and. . .

PARP!

. . .the dim glow flickered and went out. Here and there a member of Goatfield's Garden Club woke up confused, then fell into a deep, exhausted sleep. Here and there someone who had not yet been taken over sat up in their bed and said, "I'm sure I just heard a trumpet. . ."

The dogs of Smogley barked and barked, in spite of the well-aimed slippers bouncing off their heads, and all across the town the strange sounds echoed:

PARP! Toot! VUURP! PaRRUMP! **BAP!** POOOT!

* * *

Buster, Polly, Harvey and Quirke heard the distant blasts as they crept along the towpath of the old canal. That was Sanjay's French horn, echoing from among the high-rise blocks on the far side of town. There were the tuneful burps of James MacCallum's trombone and the high, bright notes of his sister's trumpet coming from outside Buster's school, and there were the others, all all right so far, tooting and parping in the back gardens out on the Smogmouth Road.

So far, so good, thought Buster, and motioned to the others to stop as Goatfield's came in sight.

He had expected the huge building to be in darkness, but it was not. From somewhere at the back a greenish shaft of light slanted into the damp night, flickering and fluttering and seeming to squirm, as if Gordon Goatfield was keeping giant glow-worms inside his garden centre.

"He must have hundreds of the things in there!" whispered Harvey.

"Maybe we should wait until morning," said Polly nervously.

"No!" said Buster. "That's what the sprouts will be expecting! By tomorrow, Gordon Goatfield will know what's happened. We've got to get in there and deal with them now, while he's not there!"

They hurried across the enormous empty car park, trying hard to look as inconspicuous as possible (and it's quite difficult to look inconspicuous at three o'clock in the morning when you're carrying a tuba and a trombone and pushing a shopping trolley containing a home-made Quirk-o-phone). Was anyone watching them from the darkened garden centre? Nobody tried to stop them; no guard dogs came snarling at them; no security-sprouts leaped out to challenge them. They ran along the outside of the wire-mesh fence that stretched around the outdoor displays. The garden centre looked so like an ordinary garden centre that Buster started to feel almost disappointed. But there was that green glow again, beckoning him on. He rounded the corner of the building, and there was a gate standing open in the fence, and an open door in the metal wall, and the green light pouring out.

"Buster, stop!" pleaded Polly. She was breathing hard, and Buster thought at first she was just puffed out from running with her heavy tuba. Then a flare of green lit up her face and he saw how scared she was. "There must be someone in there!" she said. "That door can't have been left open by accident. . ."

Buster knew she was right. "OK," he said, his heart sinking. "Harvey, Cole, we'll stop here and and have a think, all right?"

But the Quirke Brothers didn't answer, and when Buster turned to look at them he saw why. They weren't there. Now that they had seen how easily the fearsome sprouts could be destroyed they were eager to have a go themselves. They were already speeding towards the open door, both clinging to the wire sides of the shopping trolley as it careered across the gently sloping tarmac of the staff car park.

"Idiots!" hissed Buster, and he started running to catch them up.

"Buster!" he heard Polly say, lost behind him in the dark. Then there was just the quick beating of his heart and the splad-splad-splad of his trainers on the tarmac.

The Quirkes were already through the door, manoeuvring their shopping trolley into the tiny metal room beyond . . . only it wasn't a room, Buster realized as he ran in after them; it was a big lift, and Cole Quirke was already sliding the doors shut.

"Let's kick roots!" Harvey whispered excitedly.

"No!" hissed Buster. "It's not going to work! We've got to come up with another plan. . ."

"But I've just pressed the 'down' button. . ." said Cole, dismayed.

Buster felt his stomach lurch, and this time it wasn't just those annoying butterflies. The lift was dropping fast into Goatfield's basement, and the green glow from outside was getting brighter and brighter. . .

There was no going back. Buster got his trombone ready, working the slidey bit a couple of times to make sure it was nice and smooth. Cole climbed into the shopping trolley, mouth against the mouthpiece of the Quirk-o-phone, and Harvey got ready to push.

"All right," said Buster. "Remember: short, controlled blasts, and don't toot till you see the green of their tentacles. . ."

* * *

Outside, alert as a meerkat, Polly crouched in the shadows behind the garden centre and watched the green glow flare across the tarmac. What had happened to Buster? Had he caught up with the others? Why hadn't he brought them back? *Honestly*, she thought, wiping the mist off her glasses, *boys...*

And then, from somewhere beneath the garden centre she heard a burst of muffled sound; the frantic farting and parping of Buster's trombone and the deep dinosaur shudder of the Quirk-o-phone.

"Oh! Oh! Oh!" whispered Polly, fumbling her glasses back on and grabbing her tuba – but there was nothing to see, just that ominous open door and the green light.

Vuuuurp! went the distant trombone.

Plaaaaaaaaaaaaargh! boomed the Quirk-o-phone.

"What's happening to them?" Polly squeaked, glad of the sound of a friendly voice, even if it was just her own. The instruments were burping and tooting so frantically that she knew a desperate battle must have broken out under the garden centre. "If only I was there to help!" she wept.

The blasts and burbles got harder to hear. Had Buster and the others been wounded? Eaten?

Then she realized that the sounds were being drowned out by another noise, a deep rumble, a thunder that shook the ground beneath her. Buster had filled her usually-sensible brain with so many thoughts of aliens and UFOs that the first thing she thought to do was look up into the sky – but the sound was not coming from overhead. More light spilled across the car parks, headlamp-white.

Around the flank of Goatfield's Garden Centre came an enormous lorry, its air brakes hissing furiously as it backed and turned. Peering through the reflections that slid across its windscreen, Polly saw the familiar face of Gordon Goatfield. Smogley's Gardening Guru was grinning to himself as he reversed the lorry up to the open door.

* * *

Meanwhile, down in the basement, something was happening that sounded like this. . .

BAAAAAARGH! *PAROOOP!* **SNUUUURD!** *VAP!*
BADOOOOOOOOOOON!

. . .and something else was happening that sounded more like this. . .

SPLAT! GABLURSH! PLOOTCH! **SQUITTT!** **Kablooof!**

As the lift doors slid back, Buster and the Quirkes had found themselves staring at rows of metal tables, half a dozen people in Goatfield's Garden Centre dungarees and about a hundred hungry sprouts. Buster grinned and waved and groped for the "up" button, but it was too late: with shrieks and hisses and squeals the larger plants toppled from their tables and came rolling and crawling and slithering towards the open lift, and the boys had no choice but to fight. Cole blew a huge fanfare on the Quirk-o-phone, exploding two sprouts whose tentacles were already reaching for Buster's legs. Buster aimed the bell of his trombone at four smaller sprouts which came swarming across the duct-encrusted ceiling to leap down on the two brothers from above. *Vap! Vap! Vap! **PAROOP!*** Three of the plants burst apart in satisfying sprays of sludge; the fourth dropped down on to the floor of the lift.

"Buster, quick!" Harvey shouted, as the sprout's tendrils thrashed madly around at ankle level. Breathless, Buster could not use his trombone. He leaped up on to the shopping trolley and Harvey kicked off, pushing them out of the lift into the sprout-ridden basement. Cole blew a huge **THUUUUUURT!** on the Quirk-o-phone, and sprouts wilted and burst to left and right as

119

the trolley went trundling past them, knocking over tables, nearly squashing the startled garden centre staff, who were covering their ears and howling as their sprouts were splattered, before looking around in bewilderment and falling asleep.

Then the trolley's wheel skidded in a slick of sprout-juice and the whole lot toppled over, spilling out Buster, Harvey and Cole, spilling out the Quirk-o-phone, which disintegrated as it crashed on the concrete floor, leaving Cole with only the mouthpiece to blow on as the eager sprouts closed in.

PHHHHHuuurht!

One or two of the smaller sprouts shivered a bit at the sound; the rest thrashed their leaves in sprouty laughter and came on, a circle of hungry veg slowly closing around the three boys. Buster tried to use his trombone, but it was clogged with slime and bits of leaf, and as he banged it against the floor to clear it the first sticky tentacles wrapped around his arms and legs.

"We're done for!" wailed Harvey, who was being dragged upside-down into the maw of the nearest plant. "Sorry, Buster. . ."

"That's all right," said Buster, trying not to watch as another plant lifted Cole high over its open jaws and. . .

120

"Stop!" boomed a voice.

The sprouts went still, looking a bit sheepish, like children caught in the middle of a midnight raid on the biccie-barrel.

Gordon Goatfield stood at the entrance to the lift, his hands on his hips, his rosy face creased into a frown.

"Put those children down!" he told the sprouts, and one by one the tentacles holding Buster and his friends were reluctantly withdrawn.

Gordon Goatfield strutted closer, his wellies crunching and squelching through the mess on the floor. "You should know better," he told the sprouts. "You've been fed already tonight. How many times do I have to tell you that too much red meat in one night can make you grow leggy and run to seed?"

The sprouts rustled their tendrils apologetically.

"And as for you," said Gordon Goatfield, stopping in front of Buster and gripping the boy's face in his callused, gardener's hands. "I hope you're ashamed of yourself. Breaking into my garden centre. Vandalizing my property—"

"It's you who ought to be ashamed!" Buster shouted. "What do you want to go growing things like these for? You've been handing them out to your Gardening Club as if they're marigolds or

something! If it weren't for me and my friends they'd probably have taken over the whole of Smogley by now!"

"The whole of Smogley?" The Gardening Guru started to chuckle, then to laugh. "What a silly little boy you are! Do you think my plants mean to take over Smogley? What a ridiculous idea! We mean to spread our tendrils across the entire planet!"

"Oh, crikey!" whispered Harvey.

"Your stupid trumpetings have set us back a little," Gordon Goatfield admitted. "I've heard what has been going on in the town. You have splatted a lot of my seedlings, and freed their owners. But my plants will rise again! There are at least eighty left in this basement, and a truck is waiting outside ready to take specimens to every garden centre in the Greater Smogley area! Soon every gardener in Britain will be growing one of my seedlings!"

"Oh, heck!" muttered Cole.

"So what's in it for you?" demanded Buster, and as he spoke he banged the muzzle of his trombone on the floor for emphasis. "Why are you helping these things take over the world? Just so that people will be brainwashed into buying more garden stuff?" He was shouting now, making as much noise as he could in the hope that Gordon Goatfield wouldn't hear the thick squelch of the slime sliding out of his trombone. "That's the greediest thing I've ever heard!"

"Oh, I have my reasons..." said Gordon Goatfield, but before he could say what they were, Buster struck back. He swung the trombone up to his mouth and blew the loudest blast he could, driving the encircling sprouts back in a cloud of exploding slime and panic-stricken tendrils. His breath soon failed him, and he only got half a dozen of the sprouts, but in the confusion both Quirke brothers managed to slip past Gordon Goatfield and sprint towards the lift.

"Run!" shouted Buster (as if they needed telling), and started to run himself, dodging past Gordon Goatfield with a cunning manoeuvre that he had learned from years of running away from angry park-keepers and teachers.

But park-keepers and teachers, even the really angry ones, don't have seven-metre-long tentacles*. Gordon Goatfield did. The front of his blue dungarees suddenly rippled and burst and a dozen green tendrils shot out to twine round Buster's legs and bring him crashing down.

"Buster!" wailed the Quirke Brothers, reaching

* Except for Mr Kevin Pond of Class 8, Miasma Road Middle School, Chudbury – but that's another story.

back for him, but the lift was already starting to rise.

Buster struggled to get up, but the tentacles pinned him firmly to the floor and more were wrapping round him at every moment.

"Pathetic earthling!" hissed Mr Goatfield, as more leaves and tendrils uncurled from beneath his shredded clothes. "I'm not just in league with my plants — I *am* a plant!"

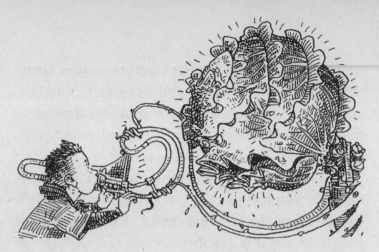

11
GREEN-FINGERED GORDON

In shopping centres and high streets, and on the better sort of bus-stop, you sometimes see those automatic advertising hoardings. Oh, you know the ones. They're made up of a lot of plastic strips, and just before you've finished looking at an advert for New Formula Squit (Washes Whiter Than Grey) they suddenly do a sort of shimmy and you find you're looking at a poster for Polly Potts's Top Notch Hot-Pots instead.

That's a bit like what Gordon Goatfield did now. He kind of folded in on himself and then folded back out again, and when he'd finished he wasn't a rosy-cheeked man in blue wellies any more – he was an enormous, angry, alien sprout in blue wellies.

Buster had seen a few weird things in his time, but as he lay trapped on the floor watching the Gardening Guru change, he quickly cleared a space at the top of his "Weird Things I Have Seen" list for a new number 1.

He also had a nasty feeling it was the Last Thing he was going to see.

Wrenching his arms free of the Goatfield-thing's tentacles, he tried one last effort to escape. "Let me go!" he shouted. "I'm warning you – I've got a trombone and I'm not afraid to use it!"

The huge sprout laughed: a rustly, rubbery sound like a tornado blowing through a bed of prize cabbages. "Try all you like, earthling! Your puny brass instruments are no match for my superior intellect!"

Buster tried a quick toot all the same, but sure enough, it had no effect on the super-sprout. A moment later a tentacle tore the trombone out of his hands and crumpled it into the shape of a question mark.

The sprout carefully took its roots out of its wellington boots. They were big, splayed roots with curving thorns all over them like claws. Now Buster understood that tub of compost in Goatfield's office, and the strange marks he had seen in it: at night, when the Gardening Guru reverted to his true form, he must plant himself there. . .

That was the only thing he did understand, though. "But how . . . what . . . why . . . where. . .???" he burbled. "How come you can look like a human being, and all the others just look like sprouts?"

The sprout sneered at him. Buster wouldn't have thought a sprout could sneer, but this one did; you couldn't mistake the way it curled its leaves. "I am fully grown," it said. "These others are just seedlings; some are old enough to leave their pots, a few are nearly ready to start mimicking you horrible animals, but the rest are still young. We take a long time to reach our final form. That is why we need you brainless creatures to serve us while we grow."

"But how did *you* grow?"

"I sprouted from a seed that had drifted through space for billions of years, clinging to a meteorite. A single seed. Luckily, when the meteorite fell here in Smogley, it was found by a man named Gordon Goatfield, a keen gardener, who took me home and carefully grew me in his greenhouse. . ."

The sprout pulled Buster close, breathing its

sprouty breath in his face. Beady eyes stared out at him from the folds of its leaves. "But Goatfield made the mistake of leaving the radio on in his greenhouse," it hissed. "He thought it would help his plants to grow! Imagine my horror, as I learned what sort of world I was sprouting in! A world ruled by animals instead of plants! A world where your people kill and eat zillions of innocent vegetables every day! You don't even make a secret of it! You have *vegetarian restaurants!*" He shivered with horror, and turned to the other sprouts and the few garden centre staff who weren't fast asleep and snoring. "Prepare the seedlings for loading! We continue as planned!" Then, turning away, he set off down the passageway and up the stairs that led to his office, dragging Buster behind him.

* * *

Out in the dark, Polly Hodge crouched behind a pile of gro-bags, peering at the activity around the huge truck. Beside her, still quivering visibly after their narrow escape from the sprouts, were the Quirke Brothers.

"We've got to go back and help Buster!" Harvey said.

"But we can't, not with those people coming in

and out all the time," said Cole. "What are they doing anyway?"

"They're loading that lorry with seedlings!" whispered Polly, as another batch of sprouts was wheeled out of the lift and packed carefully into the truck.

"They're getting ready to send them off to other towns!" said Harvey. "And once they're grown they'll start impersonating people, like Mr Goatfield."

"They'll probably impersonate the Prime Minister first," said Cole helpfully. "That's what I'd do, if I was an alien plant. And the Queen, and all the top generals and air force blokes, so nobody can stop them."

"Will you two SHUT UP!" shouted Polly, who was so worried about Buster that she forgot for a moment they were deep in enemy territory. Luckily, her shout was drowned out by the sound of the truck's big doors slamming shut. The loading was complete. The garden centre staff wandered back inside, leaving one man outside to guard the lorry.

"I expect they've gone to get Gordon Goatfield," said Polly. "He was driving it earlier – he probably doesn't trust those zombies to deliver his seedlings safely." Then an idea struck her. "I know! Harvey, Cole, can you distract that guard?"

"I think so," said Harvey.

"I'm sure of it," said Cole, pulling out his Squirtmaster Gloosh-o-matic.

"Then do it; and when you've finished, go and find Lindsay and Sanjay and the others." She hefted her tuba. "I'm going to deal with that truck; and then I'm going to rescue Buster!"

The man who had been left on guard beside the lorry was called Percy Smalls, and he was having a strange night. His own seedling had survived the battle in the basement, and was safe aboard the lorry now, so he was still a slave to the sprouts, but the toots and trumpetings had given him a headache. Somewhere in the back of his mind an idea was starting to form that this wasn't what he'd expected to be doing when he replied to the advert about jobs in the new garden centre. Percy wondered if he had made a mistake when he gave up his old job as a milkman. He couldn't quite put his finger on it, but something funny was definitely going on at this Goatfield's place. . .

Suddenly two powerful jets of water came glooshing out of the darkness and splattered against his face, startling him so much that he fell sideways, crashing into the truck. He heard the sprouts inside rustling angrily. In the darkness at the edge of the car park two small shapes went scurrying away.

"Oi!" shouted Percy, giving chase. "You kids! Come back here!"

Behind him a plump figure hurried up to the truck and placed the bell of her tuba against one of the air-vents low down on the rear door. There was an enormous, thundering **THWAAAAARP!**

Percy Smalls fell over, clutching his ears, and Polly kept her tuba against the vent and played three more notes, feeling the lorry rock with the sound, hearing the hiss and splatter as the sprouts inside exploded. She gave them a quick blast of Mozart's G-flat horn concerto, just for luck.

Percy stood up, looking about in bewilderment. He could hear the echoes of a tuba dying away. He could see green goo dribbling out of the air-vents of the lorry, and the girl running away into the garden centre. He just wasn't sure how he came to be there, or what he had been doing.

It was so confusing that he sat down and went to sleep. In his dreams, his turbo-powered milk float won the Silverstone Grand Prix, the Paris-Dakkar rally and the America's Cup yacht race, and he snuggled down comfortably on the tarmac, deciding that tomorrow he'd go back to his old job.

From inside the garden centre came a few quick, muffled parps as Polly dealt with the last of the sprouts in the basement, and set off to search for Buster.

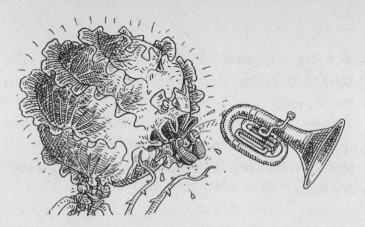

12
CROUCHING TUBA,
HIDDEN SPROUT

"So what happened to the real Mr Goatfield?" asked Buster awkwardly, his face squashed against the sprout's leaves as it lugged him up the stairs.

"I ate him, of course," said the sprout. "Then I used his money to open this garden centre; a place where I could grow more of my kind without raising anyone's suspicions. Luckily, you humans have a fatal weakness; the pathetic hobby you call *gardening*." He sniggered, twitching his tendrils. "My Gardening Club was just an experiment, to see if I could persuade humans to nurture us until there are enough of us to take over this planet. And it was a huge success! Your tiny human brains are almost too easy to control. . ."

"Until you get a blast of trombone music," said Buster, as the sprout hauled him through the boiler-room door into Mr Goatfield's office. "It's going to be a bit difficult taking over the world if you go off splat every time you hear a brass band."

"Huh!" sniffed the sprout. "I admit I had not reckoned with those disgusting sound-making devices. But as long as we are protected from their vibrations in our early form we can learn to endure them. Look!" He reached over to the desk and picked up his walkman, clamping the headphones over Buster's ears. The oompah music which burst out when he pressed the start button was so loud that even Buster felt a bit like exploding.

"It's called *The Best Brass Band Album in the Whole Wide World Ever, Honest!*" shouted the sprout, tapping his roots in time to the music. "I started with tiny bursts at the lowest possible volume, and gradually increased the dosage. Now I can listen to the whole record at full blast, with barely any ill effects at all!" Mad laughter rippled the sprout's leaves, and Buster felt his last hope slip away. If this thing was immune to brass bands, how on earth could he fight it?

Hoping to reason with it he said, "Look, Mr Goatfield, or whatever you call yourself, maybe you're going at this the wrong way. If you talked to people and told them how you feel about them eating vegetables and all, maybe they'd understand. We're not *all* vegetarians, you know. I mostly eat biscuits. I'd hardly eat vegetables at all if Mum didn't make me. I'm not your enemy. . ."

"Oh, I don't think of you as my enemy," said the sprout kindly. Then its thorn-lined mouth gaped wide. "I think of you as a tasty snack!"

"Buster!"

Buster had been almost eaten so many times that night that he was starting to get quite used to it, but it was still a relief when Fake Cousin Polly's voice came echoing through the silent garden centre.

"Buster!" she called. "Where are you?"

The Sprout Formerly Known As Gordon Goatfield lowered Buster and turned to rip the door off its hinges, beady eyes blinking out into the dark. "Guards!" he shouted, but Polly's tuba had finished off the last of the sprouts and his staff were all fast asleep. Rustling his leaves, he stepped out of the office.

In the dim glow of the night-lighting the indoor plant section looked like a dense jungle.

Polly crept through it, a Quirke Brother's head-torch strapped to her brow, her tuba at the ready. A noise from the direction of the office made her spin round. She was as alert as a meerkat who suspects its friends are planning to throw it a surprise birthday party. "Buster?"

Still tangled in Gordon Goatfield's tentacles, Buster shouted, "Polly! Watch out! Goatfield's coming! He's a super-sprout, and he's—" but before he could say, "immune to tuba music" another tentacle clamped across his mouth. From somewhere in the indoor plant section came the throaty bellow of a tuba. The giant sprout swung towards it, tendrils twitching. Then, instead of diving into the mass of leaves and shadows as Buster had expected, it suddenly turned and ran straight up the wall, gripping the ducts and pipes above with its roots and tendrils. Upside down, it scuttled across the ceiling like an enormous spider, looking down between the aisles of potted plants.

Polly was creeping towards the information desk. It never occurred to her to look up, and the sprout made sure that Buster could not call out a warning. As she reached the desk it suddenly dropped from the roof and landed next to her, startling her so much that she couldn't find the breath to blow her tuba. A dozen tentacles lashed out, gripped her, and lifted her into the sprout's green maw.

"Eeeeeeeep!" squealed Polly, her feet kicking frantically between the gaping leaves.

"Yummy!" belched the sprout, and swallowed her whole, spitting out the tuba, which splashed into a nearby ornamental pond.

"Polly!" wailed Buster, trying not to believe what had just happened.

"Now for seconds!" chuckled the sprout, untangling the tentacles which held Buster and lifting him by his legs. "Yes," it chuckled, "quake in terror, feeble human! Now you know how one of your earth chips feels when you cover it in bludgeoned tomatoes and stuff it into your mouth! Now you know what a poor innocent carrot must go through when you skin it alive and drop it into boiling water! Now you know. . ."

Thank heavens for monsters who gloat over their victims, thought Buster. The sprout's speechifying gave him just enough time to press the headphones of Gordon Goatfield's walkman against the microphone on the information desk, switch on the loudspeaker controls, wrench the volume knob to FULL and press PLAY.

The sound that came rolling out of the garden

centre's loudspeaker system was so loud that it hardly sounded like sound at all; it filled Buster's whole mind, tinny and crackly and distorted, but still recognizable as *In an English Country Garden* performed by the Massed Bands of the Grenadier Guards.

The super-sprout certainly recognized it. It dropped Buster, who fell in a heap behind the control desk. **AIEEEE!** it bellowed. It thrashed its tentacles about, trying to reach for the loudspeaker controls, but the thunderous noise and the vibrations were too much for it. **AUUUUERRRGH!** The veins of its rubbery leaves swelled and throbbed, its tendrils wilted, its leaves crumpled, its roots curled, and. . .

Buster rose carefully from behind the desk, wiping the sticky goo out of his eyes. When he turned off the tape, the silence sounded even louder than the noise that had come before it. All he could hear was his own thudding heart, and the thick *plip, plop* as pieces of sprout dripped from the ceiling.

"Oh, Polly. . ." he whispered, wondering what

on earth he was going to tell Fake Auntie Pauline and Fake Uncle Tim.

Then he saw her. She was sitting where the sprout had stood, dripping with sludge and looking very surprised at having been eaten and even more surprised to be safe again.

Buster gave a whoop of delight and vaulted over the information desk to help her up. She was shaking with fright and feeling sick from all the sprout-slime she had swallowed. She was also terribly glad to see Buster alive – but she wasn't going to let him see any of that. "Oh, hello Buster," she said casually.

Buster just grinned at her, quite certain that he had the coolest Fake Cousin in the whole world ever.

* * *

Outside, dawn was coming up beyond the flyover and the hum and clatter of a distant milk float echoed across the housing estates. As Polly and Buster walked out into the grey light they saw the others coming to meet them across the car park; tired, happy, covered in bits of sprout, breaking into a run as they recognized their friends. For a while they all hugged each other and danced about, swapping stories of their adventures.

"I think we got them all," said Lindsay Spratt.

"There are none left up at the school," said Katie MacCallum, "James and me made sure of that! We tooted outside every window, and even in Mr Creaber's greenhouse. . ."

"The allotments are clear," reported Henry Hill.

"And the Smogmouth Road," agreed Sanjay.

"A great big one crawled out of a cold frame, right at me!" Belinda told them, still giggling with fright and excitement. "I gave it a couple of bars of *Colonel Bogey*. You should've seen it splatter!"

Buster looked round happily at them; these musical types weren't nearly as weird or sad as he had thought; in fact, they were almost like normal people. Who would have thought he would end up being friends with the school orchestra? "But we can't be too careful," he reminded them. "There might be one or two left, in a greenhouse or a porch or on a garden window sill somewhere. It's going to be up to us. If we hear of anybody's auntie acting strangely, or anybody's dad spending too much time in the greenhouse, we'll know what to do. . ."

"And watch the flowerpots," agreed Polly. "At home, at school, at your friends' houses. Keep watching the flowerpots. . ."

They walked home, feeling sadder and sadder

as one by one the members of the Anti-Sprout Squad said goodbye and went off towards their own homes. At last it was time for even the Quirke Brothers to go. "No more monster hunting for us!" said Harvey, waving goodbye.

"We're going to find a safer way to earn pocket money," agreed Cole. "We might open a detective agency. . ."

"Or dig for buried treasure," suggested his brother.

"Or build a spaceship. . ."

"Or become ace cat-burglars and steal the Spudsylvanian Crown Jewels."

"There's no such place."

"Yes, there is."

"Isn't."

"Is."

"You're making it up. . ."

The sound of their bickering voices faded into the distance, and Buster and Polly went on in silence, walking the last few blocks to Acacia Crescent. Smogley was strangely quiet, the burr of rush-hour traffic from the flyover muted. Here and there, a splat of crusty green sludge showed on the inside of a greenhouse. Cars stood silently on forecourts, waiting for their owners to sleep off the effects of the space-sprouts' mind control.

Fake Auntie Pauline and Fake Uncle Tim were awake, bustling dazedly about in the kitchen, making tea. The TV was on, and a chirpy announcer was saying. *"We're getting reports from Smogley about a spate of hit-and-run trumpet recitals which shook the town in the early hours of this morning. Practical jokers seem to be responsible for the mystery music – and a number of householders are claiming that their porches and conservatories have been splattered with what appears to be cold sprout soup! We asked a spokesman for Smogley Police to comment, but apparently he's still fast asleep. . ."*

"Disgraceful," muttered Fake Auntie Pauline, clutching her head.

"Just some kids mucking about, I expect," said Fake Uncle Tim weakly. Neither of them had any memories at all of the last few days, but they both had terrible headaches. They didn't want any of the monster breakfast that Buster and Polly started making as soon as they had washed and changed out of their sprout-sploshed clothes. "Were we at a party last night?" asked Fake Auntie Pauline suspiciously. "I feel as though I may have had a little too much to drink. I do hope I didn't do anything silly. . ."

"I'm sure you'd never do anything silly,

Mummy," said Polly loyally.

Buster was just finishing his fifth slice of toast and honey when the doorbell bonged. He ran to the front door and flung it open and there was Mum, back from Belgium, with a Camp Kludge fleece for Polly and a nice, ordinary, non-man-eating plant for Fake Auntie Pauline. "Steady, Buster!" she laughed, as Buster hugged her. "I haven't been away *that* long! I see Pauline's redecorating the front of her house again. Sprout green, eh? Very fashionable. . . So how's your stay been?"

Buster opened his mouth to tell her. Then he decided that perhaps there were some things mums weren't meant to know.

"Oh, you know," he said. "Boring."

THE END?